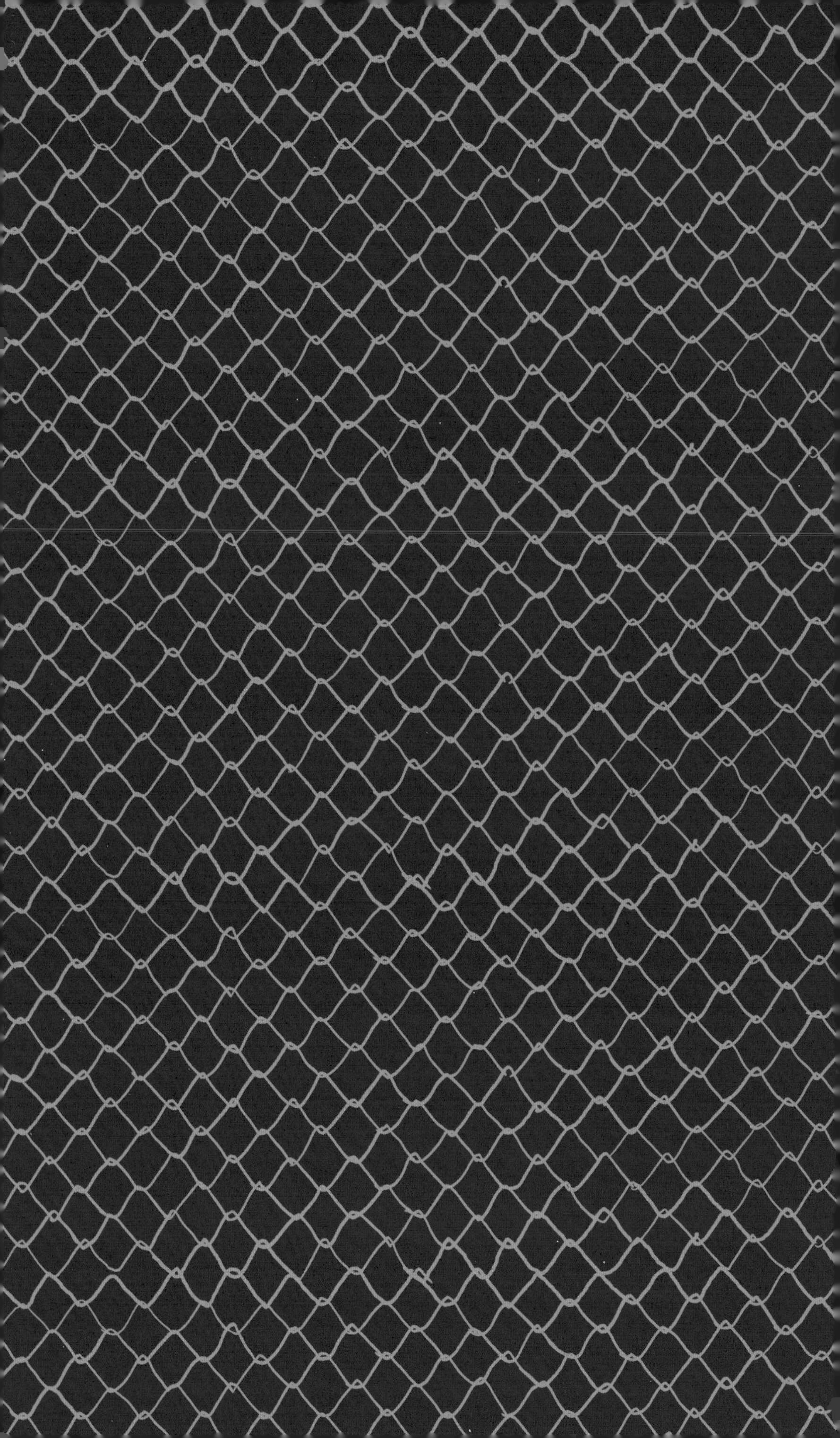

Epigram

Oh, it must be something I did in the past.
Don't it just make you wanna laugh?

"Goodnight, Ladies"
Lou Reed (1972)

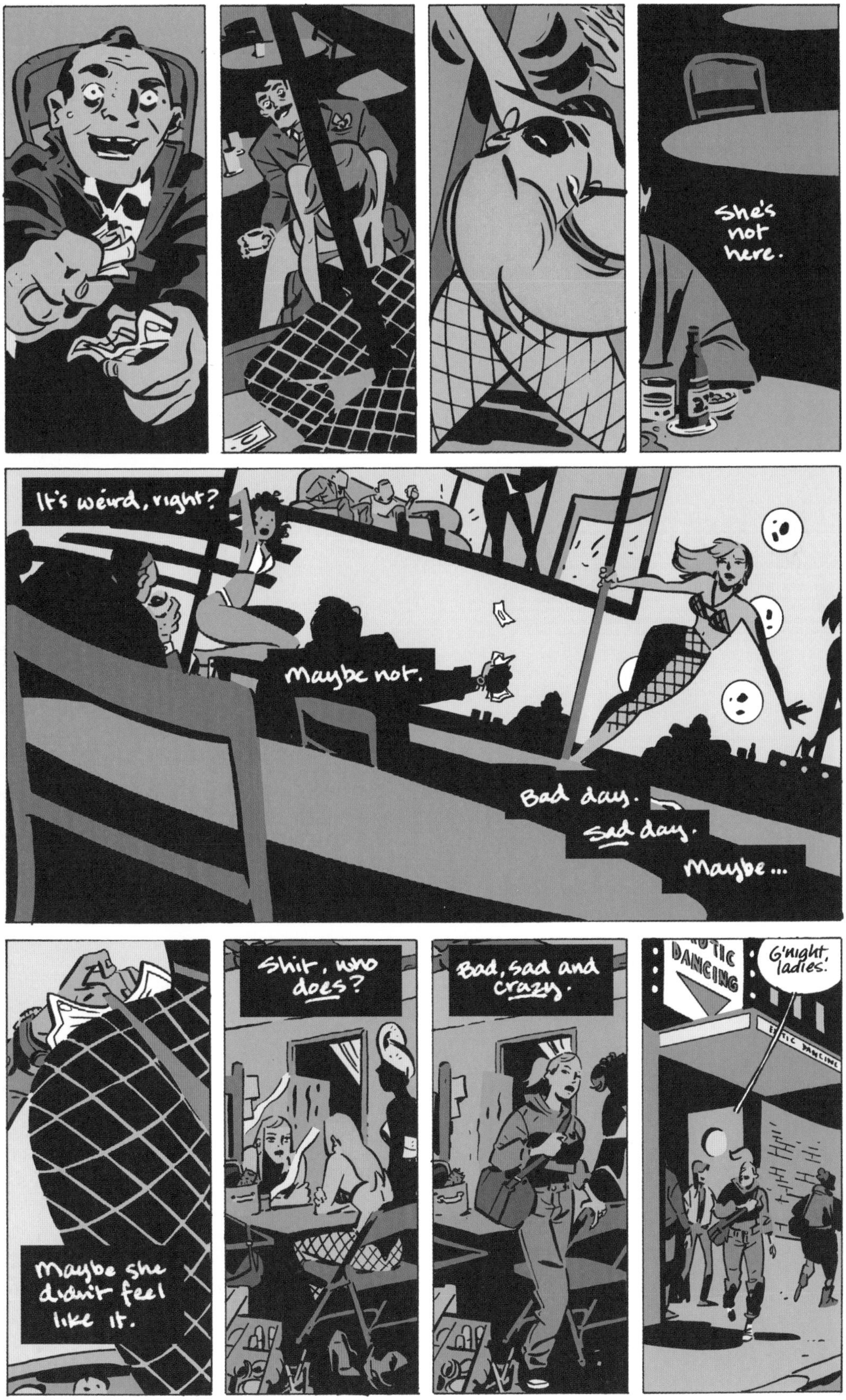
She's not here.
It's weird, right?
Maybe not.
Bad day.
Sad day.
Maybe...
Maybe she didn't feel like it.
Shit, who does?
Bad, sad and crazy.
EROTIC DANCING
G'night, ladies!

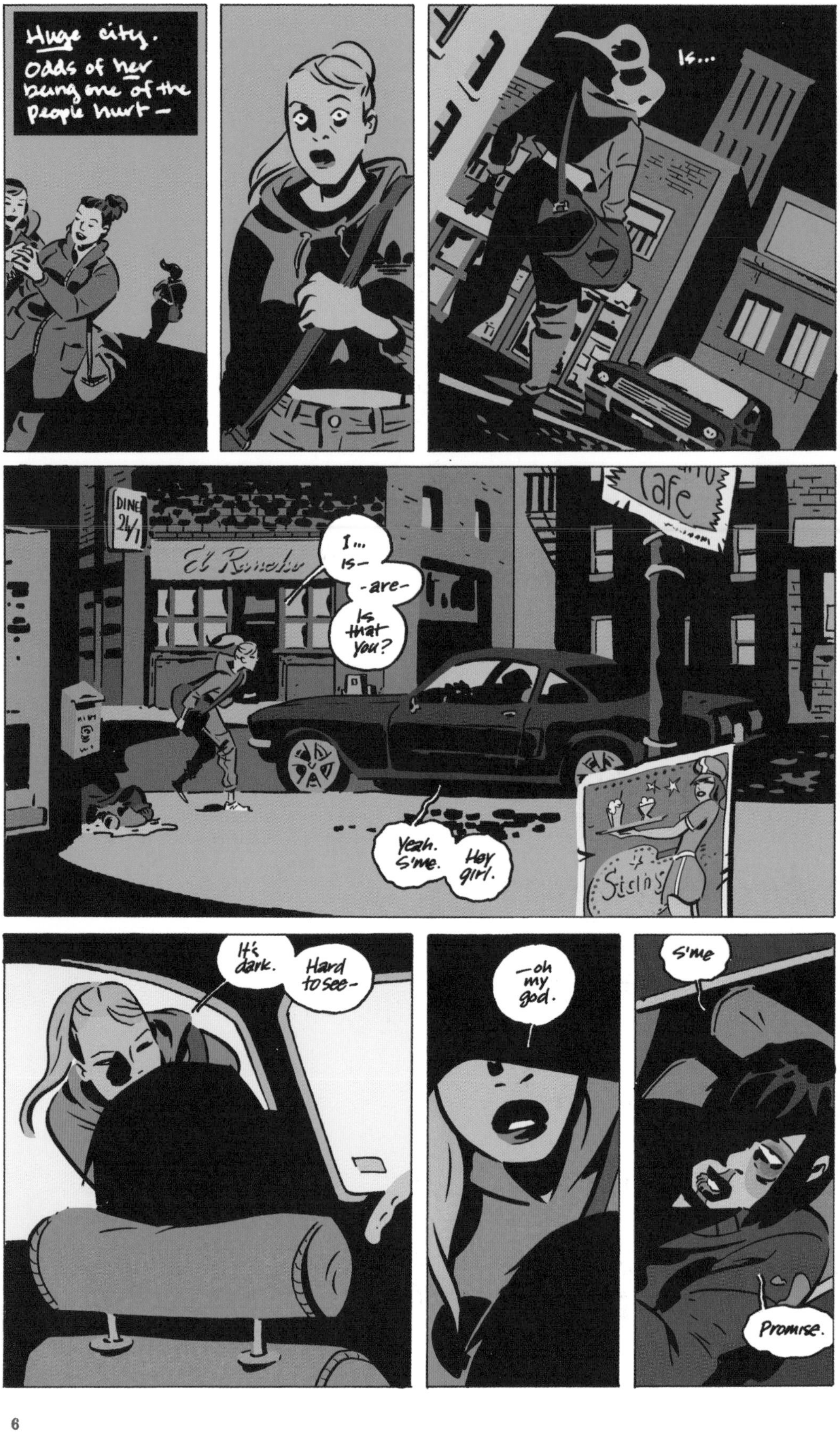
Huge city.
Odds of her being one of the people hurt —
Is...
DINER 24/7
El Rancho
Cafe
I...
Is—
-are-
Is that you?
Yeah. S'me.
Hey girl.
It's dark.
Hard to see-
—oh my god.
S'me
Promise.

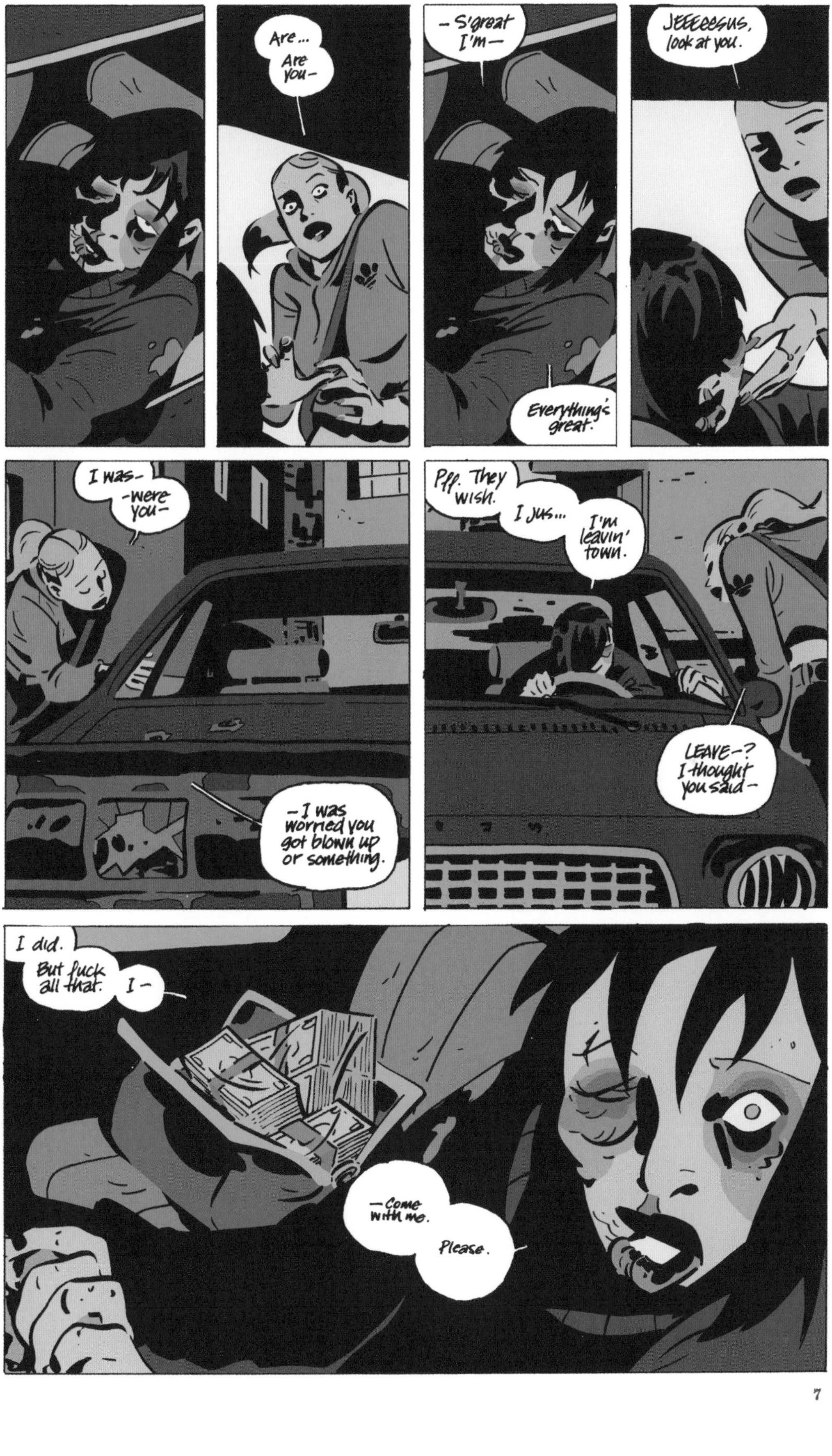
Are...
Are you-
- S'great I'm-
Everything's great.
JEEEeesus, look at you.
I was-
-were you-
-I was worried you got blown up or something.
Pff. They wish.
I jus...
I'm leavin' town.
LEAVE-? I thought you said-
I did.
But fuck all that.
I-
-Come with me.
Please.

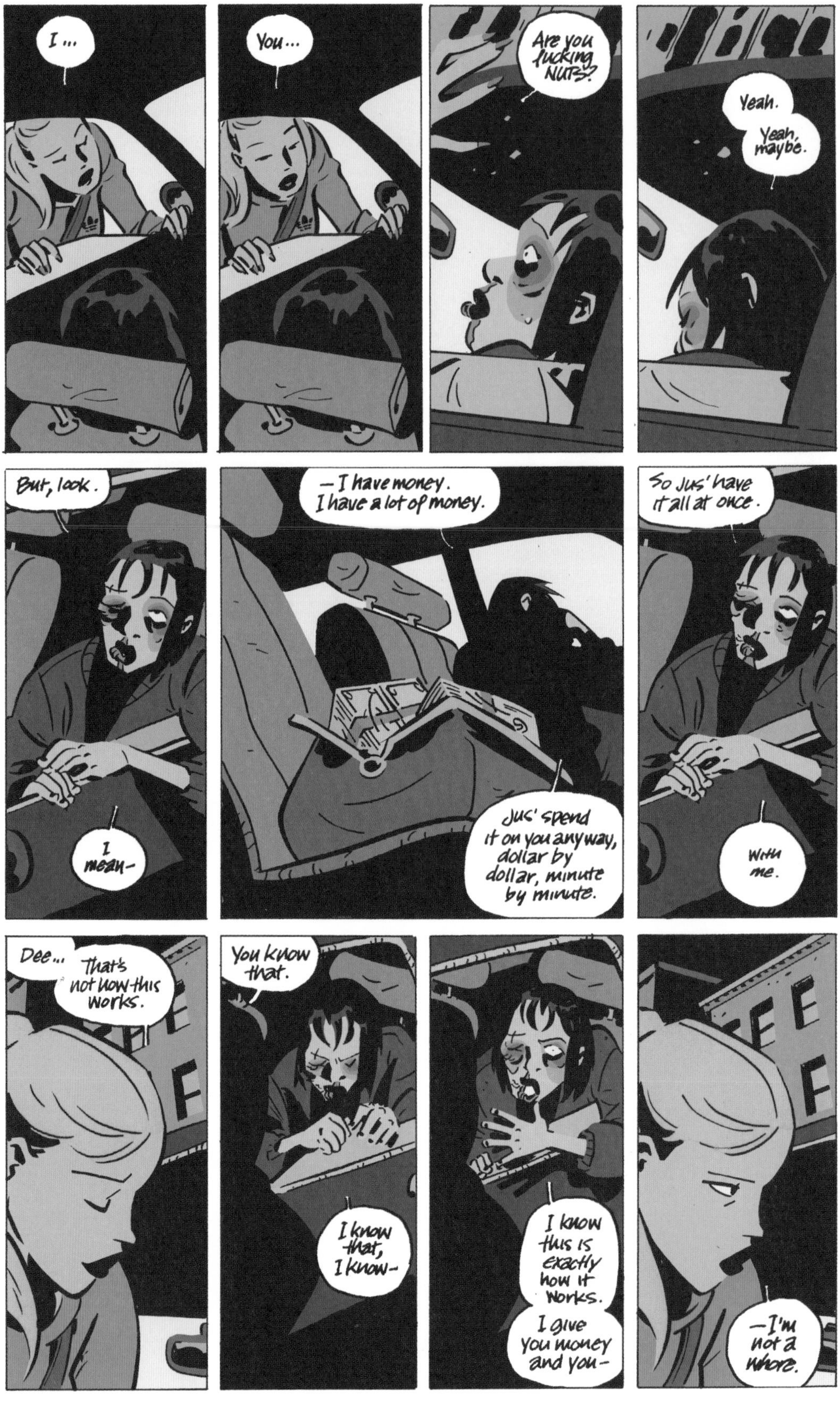
I...
You...
Are you fucking NUTS?
Yeah.
Yeah, maybe.
But, look.
I mean-
—I have money. I have a lot of money.
Jus' spend it on you anyway, dollar by dollar, minute by minute.
So jus' have it all at once.
With me.
Dee...
That's not how this works.
You know that.
I know that, I know-
I know this is exactly how it works.
I give you money and you-
—I'm not a whore.

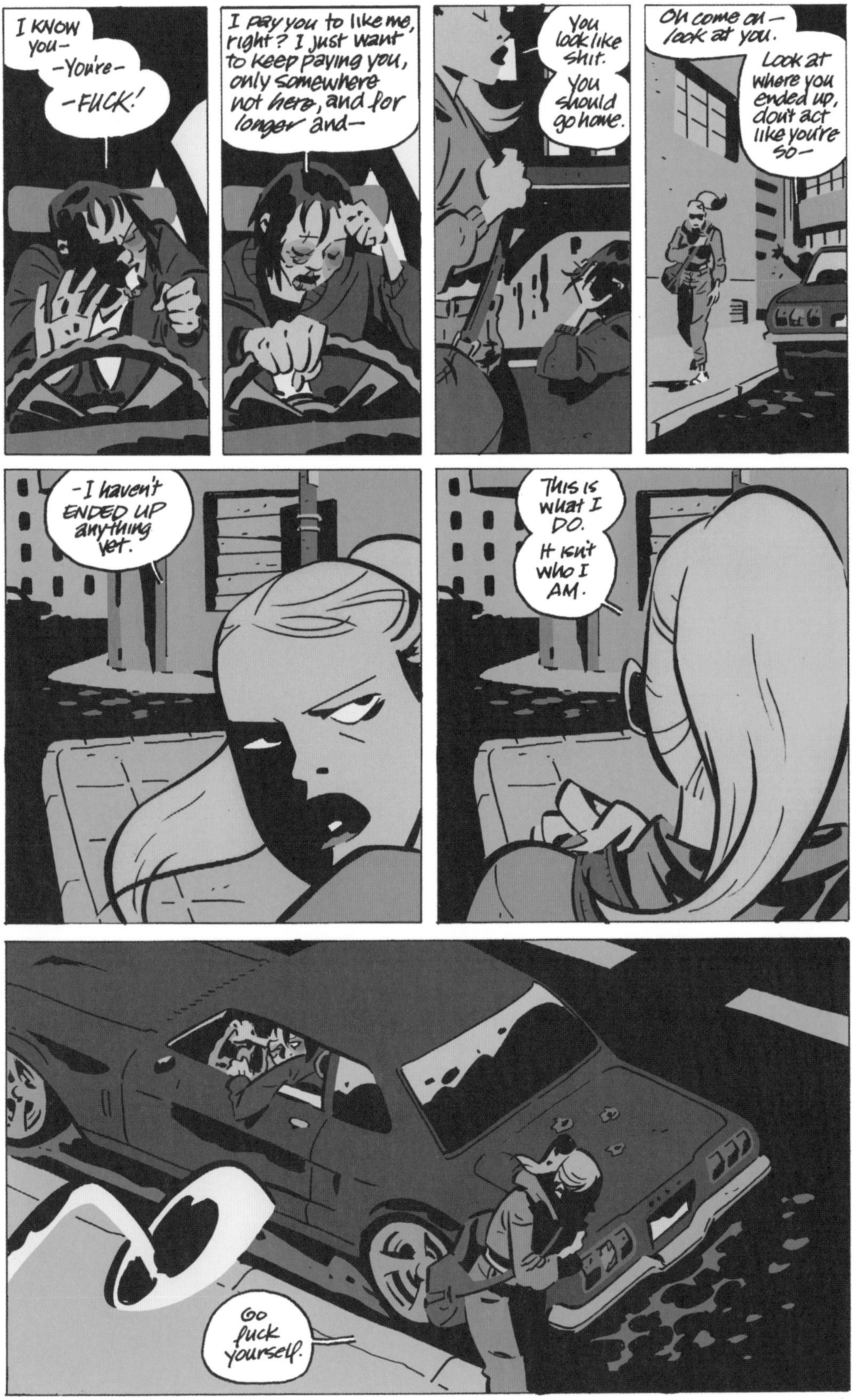
I KNOW you-
-You're-
-FUCK!
I pay you to like me, right? I just want to keep paying you, only somewhere not here, and for longer and-
You look like shit.
You should go home.
Oh come on- look at you.
Look at where you ended up, don't act like you're so-
-I haven't ENDED UP anything yet.
This is what I DO.
It isn't who I AM.
Go fuck yourself.

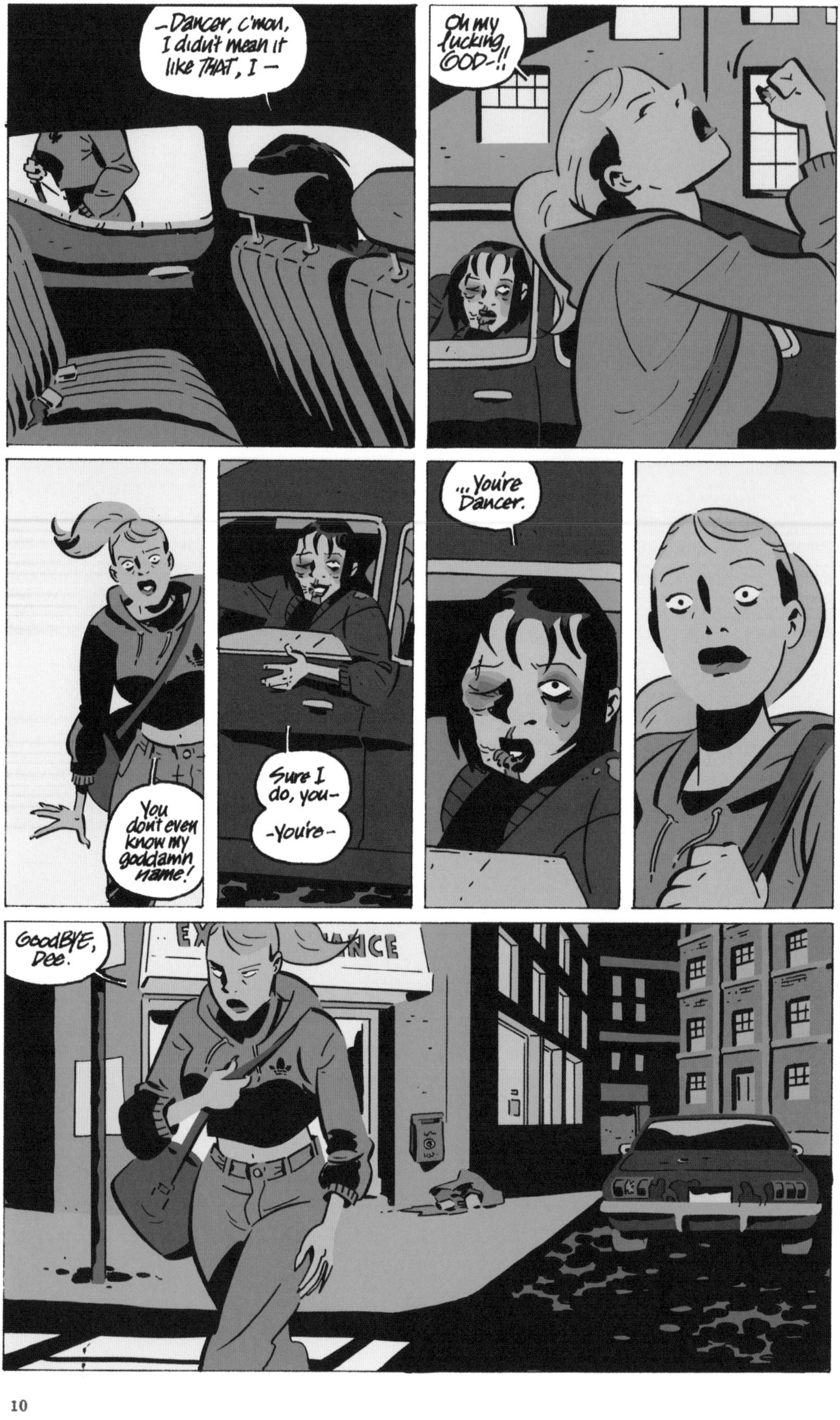

-Dancer, c'mon, I didn't mean it like THAT, I —
Oh my fucking GOD-!!
You don't even know my goddamn name!
Sure I do, you-
-You're-
...You're Dancer.
GoodBYE, Dee.

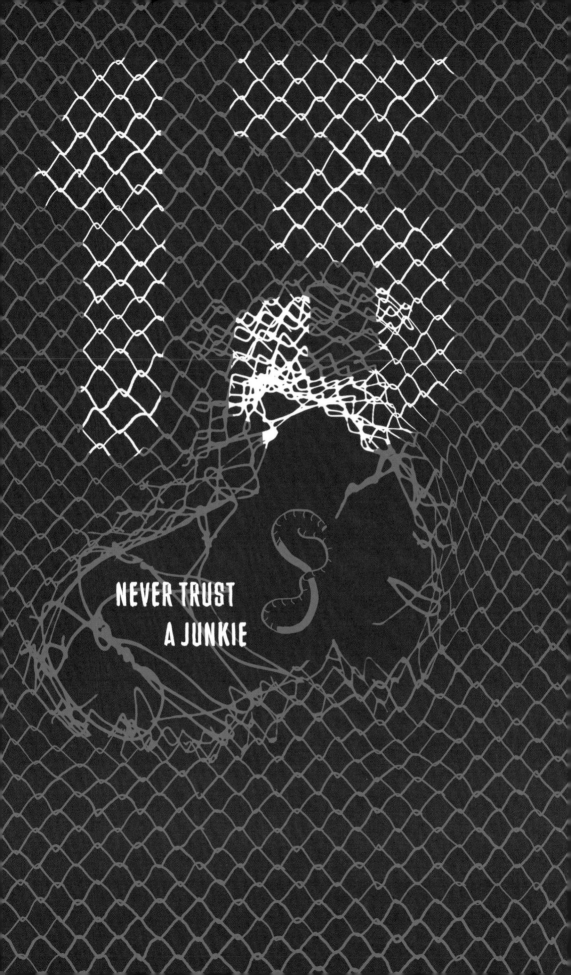

NEVER TRUST
A JUNKIE

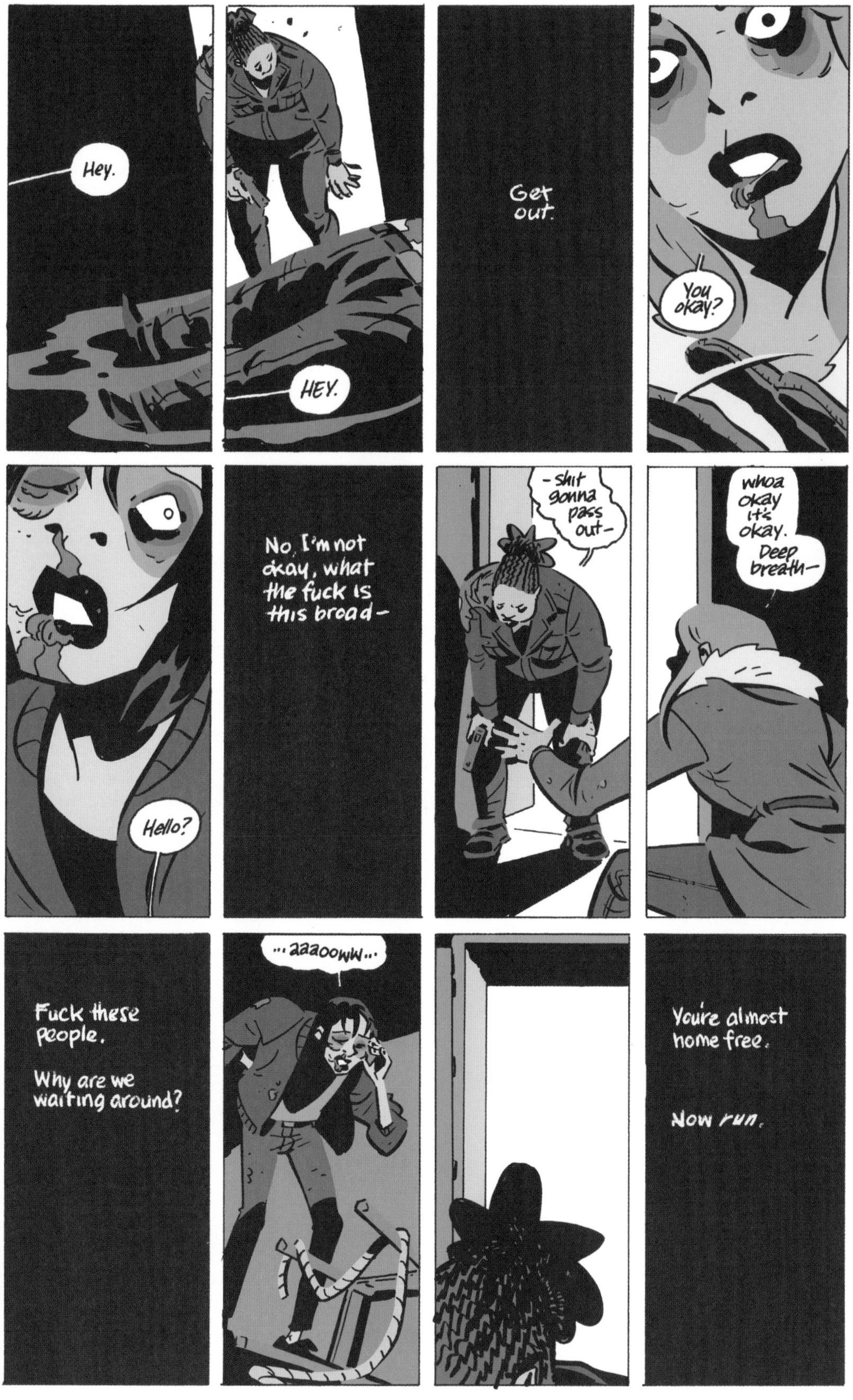
Hey.
HEY.
Get out.
You okay?
Hello?
No, I'm not okay, what the fuck is this broad-
-shit gonna pass out-
whoa okay it's okay. Deep breath-
Fuck these people.
Why are we waiting around?
...aaaoowW...
You're almost home free.
Now run.

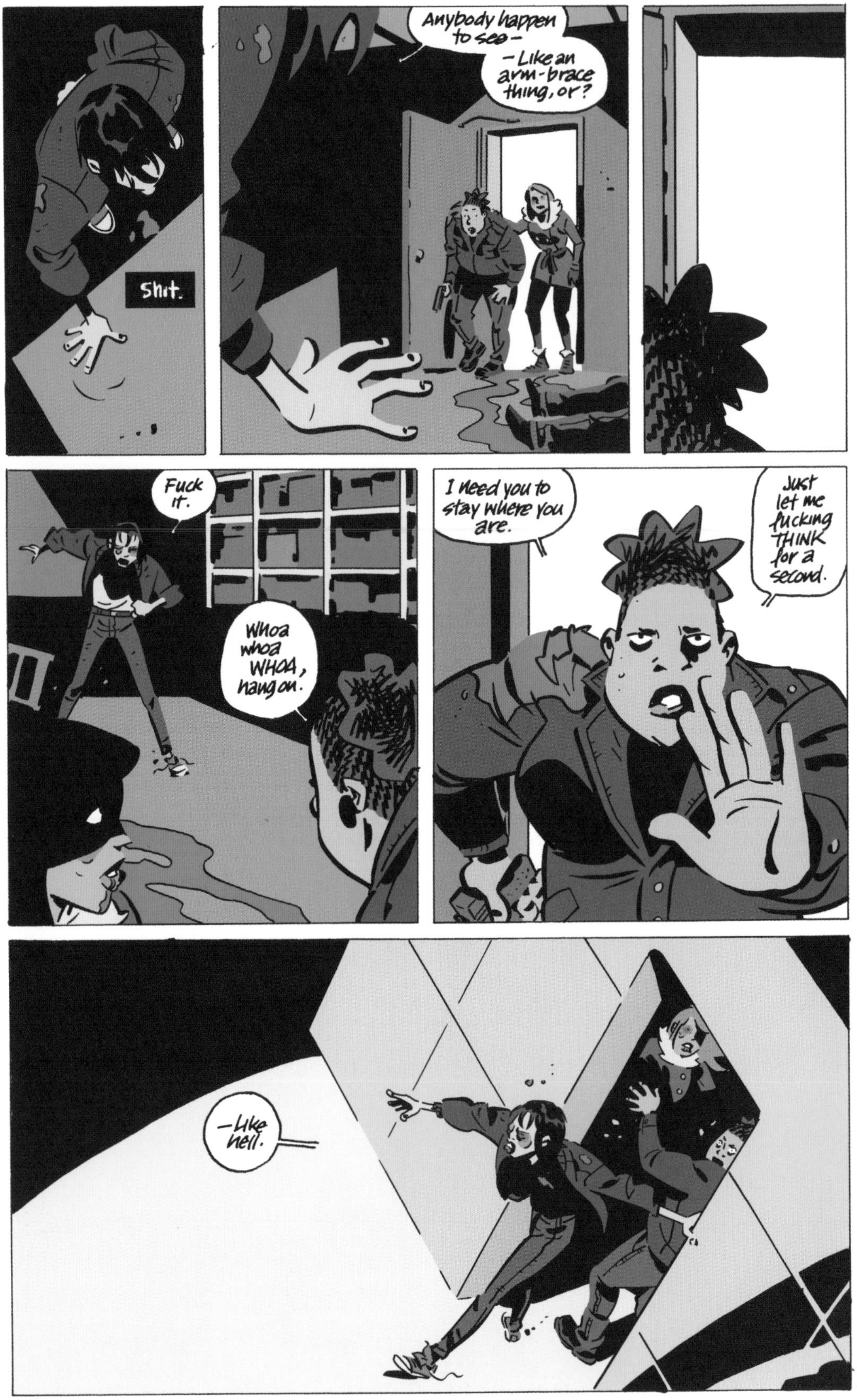
Shit.
Anybody happen to see—
—Like an arm-brace thing, or?
Fuck it.
Whoa whoa WHOA, hang on.
I need you to stay where you are.
Just let me fucking THINK for a second.
—Like hell.

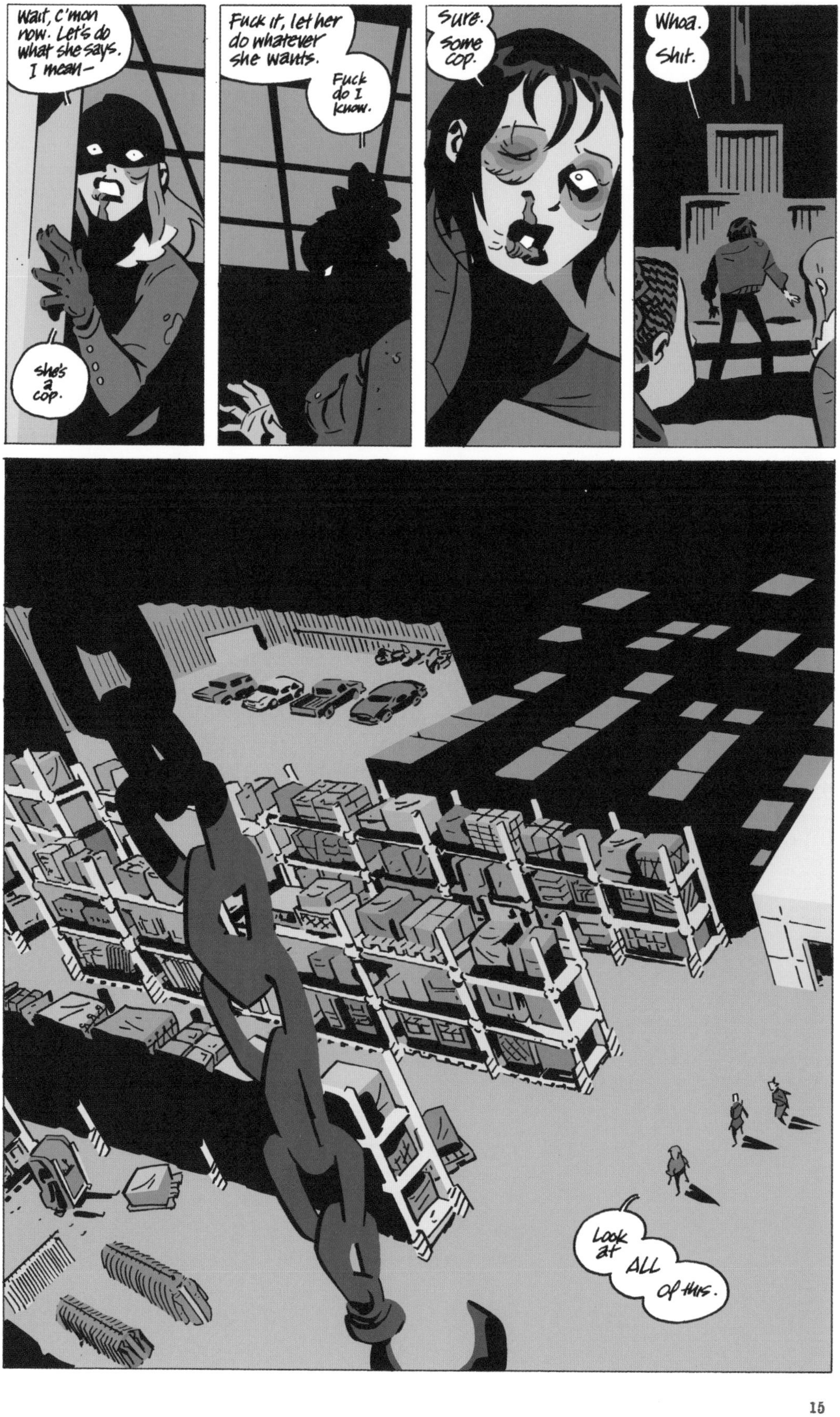
Wait, c'mon now. Let's do what she says. I mean—
she's a cop.
Fuck it, let her do whatever she wants.
Fuck do I know.
Sure.
Some cop.
Whoa.
Shit.
Look at ALL of this.

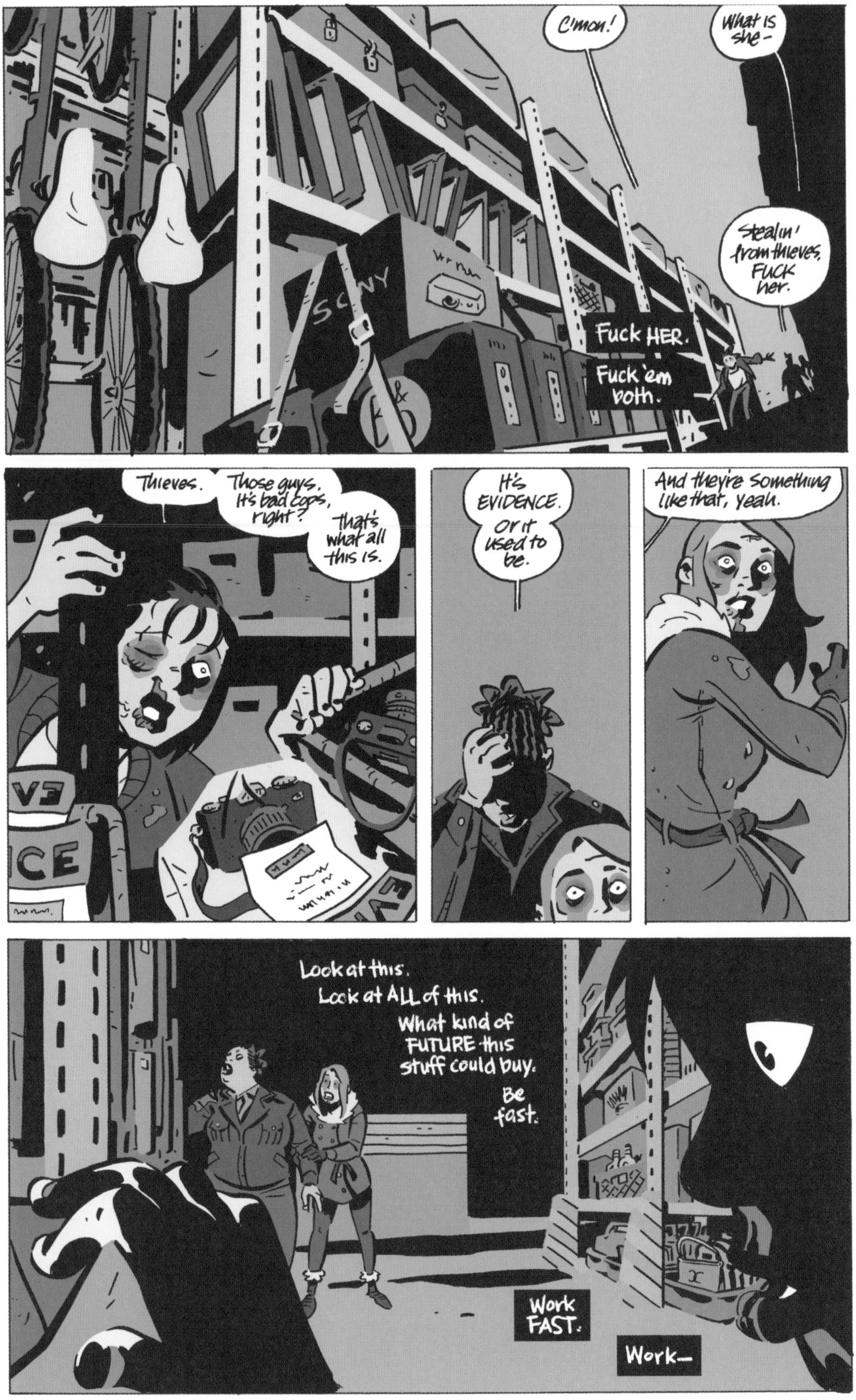
C'mon!
What is she-
Stealin' from thieves. Fuck her.
Fuck HER.
Fuck 'em both.
Thieves.
Those guys. It's bad cops, right?
That's what all this is.
It's EVIDENCE. Or it used to be.
And they're something like that, yeah.
Look at this.
Look at ALL of this.
What kind of FUTURE this stuff could buy.
Be fast.
Work FAST.
Work—

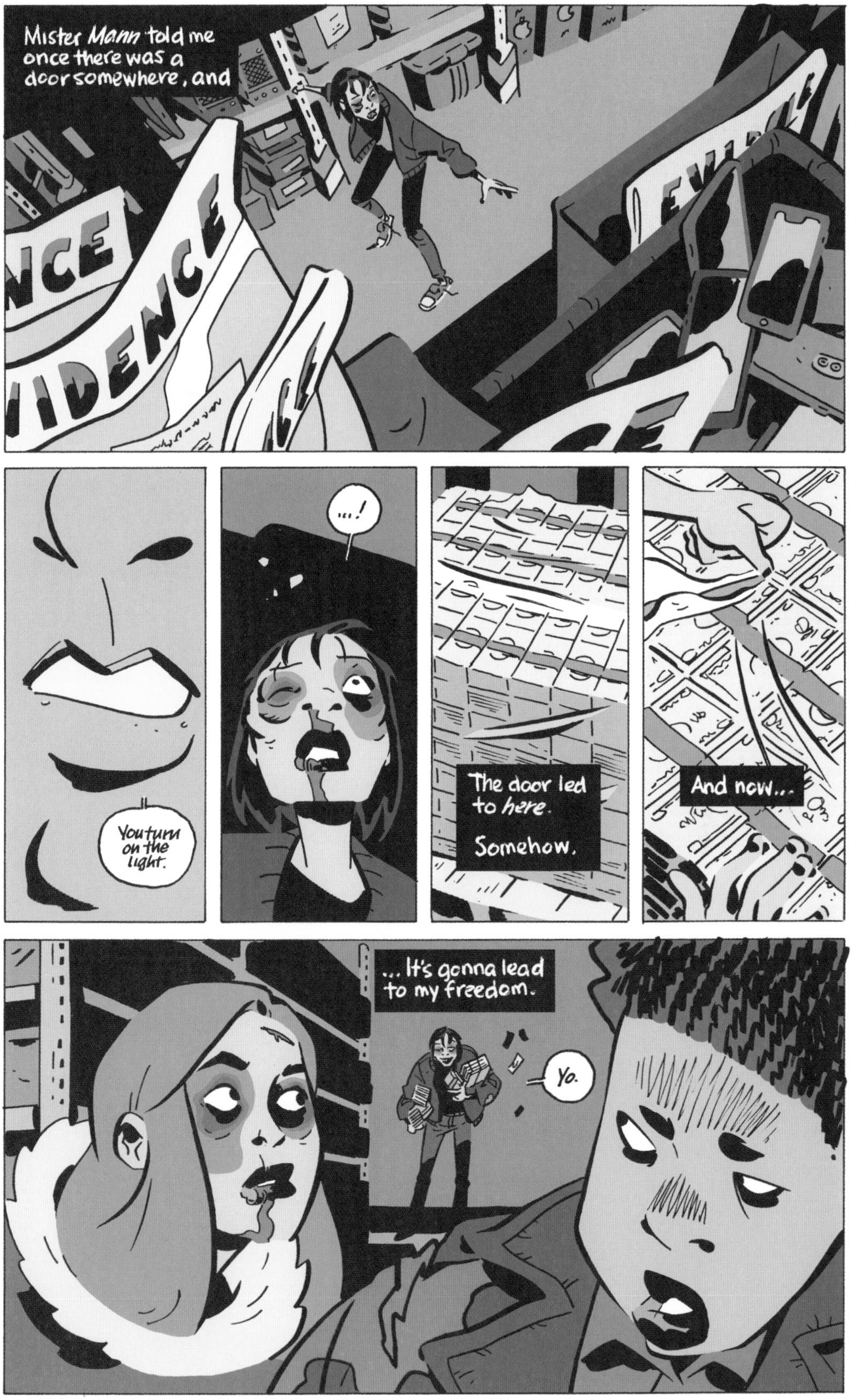
Mister Mann told me once there was a door somewhere, and
EVIDENCE
You turn on the light.
...!
The door led to here.
Somehow.
And now...
... It's gonna lead to my freedom.
Yo.

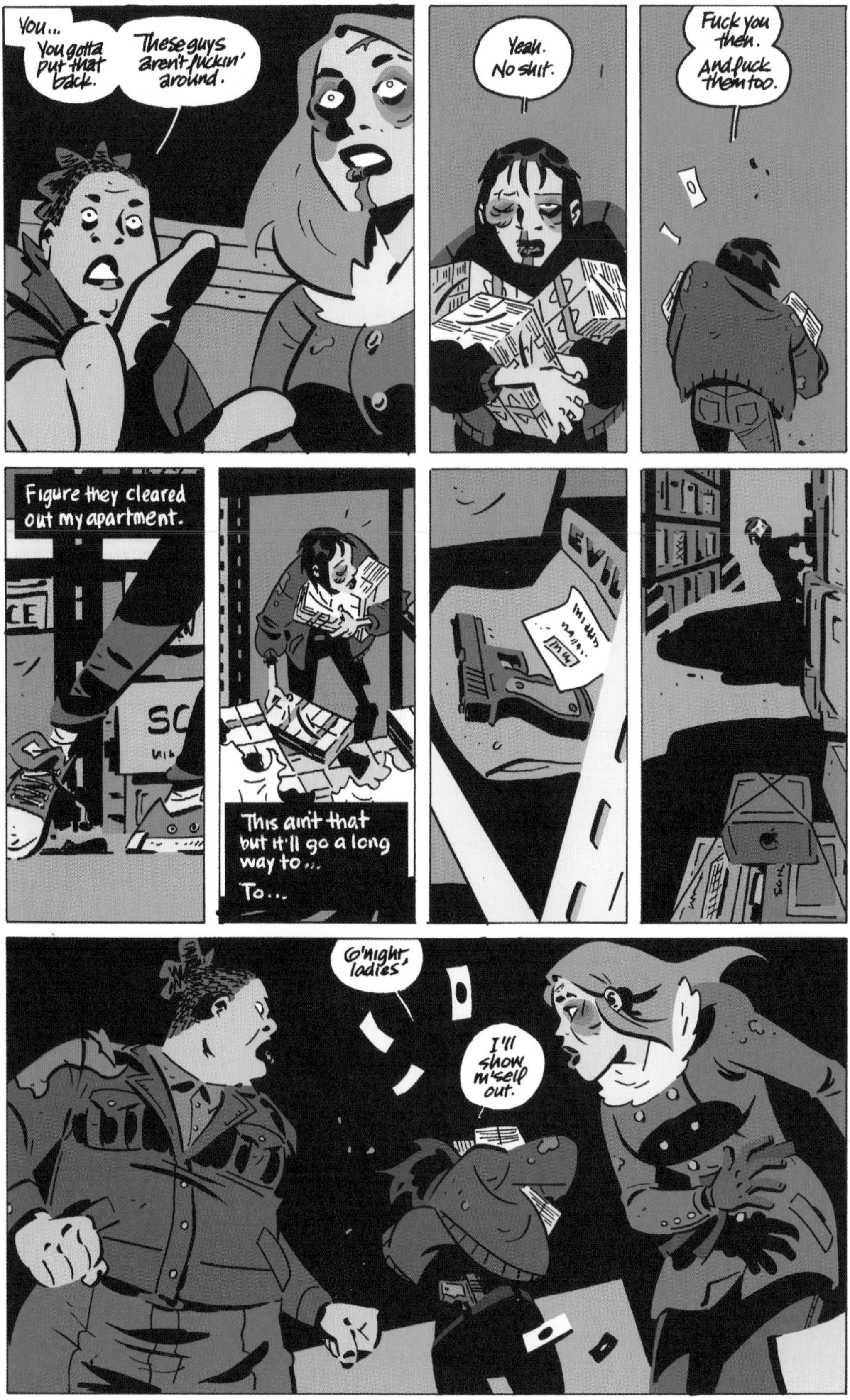
You... You gotta put that back.
These guys aren't fuckin' around.
Yeah. No shit.
Fuck you then. And fuck them too.
Figure they cleared out my apartment.
This ain't that but it'll go a long way to...
To...
G'night, ladies'
I'll show m'self out.

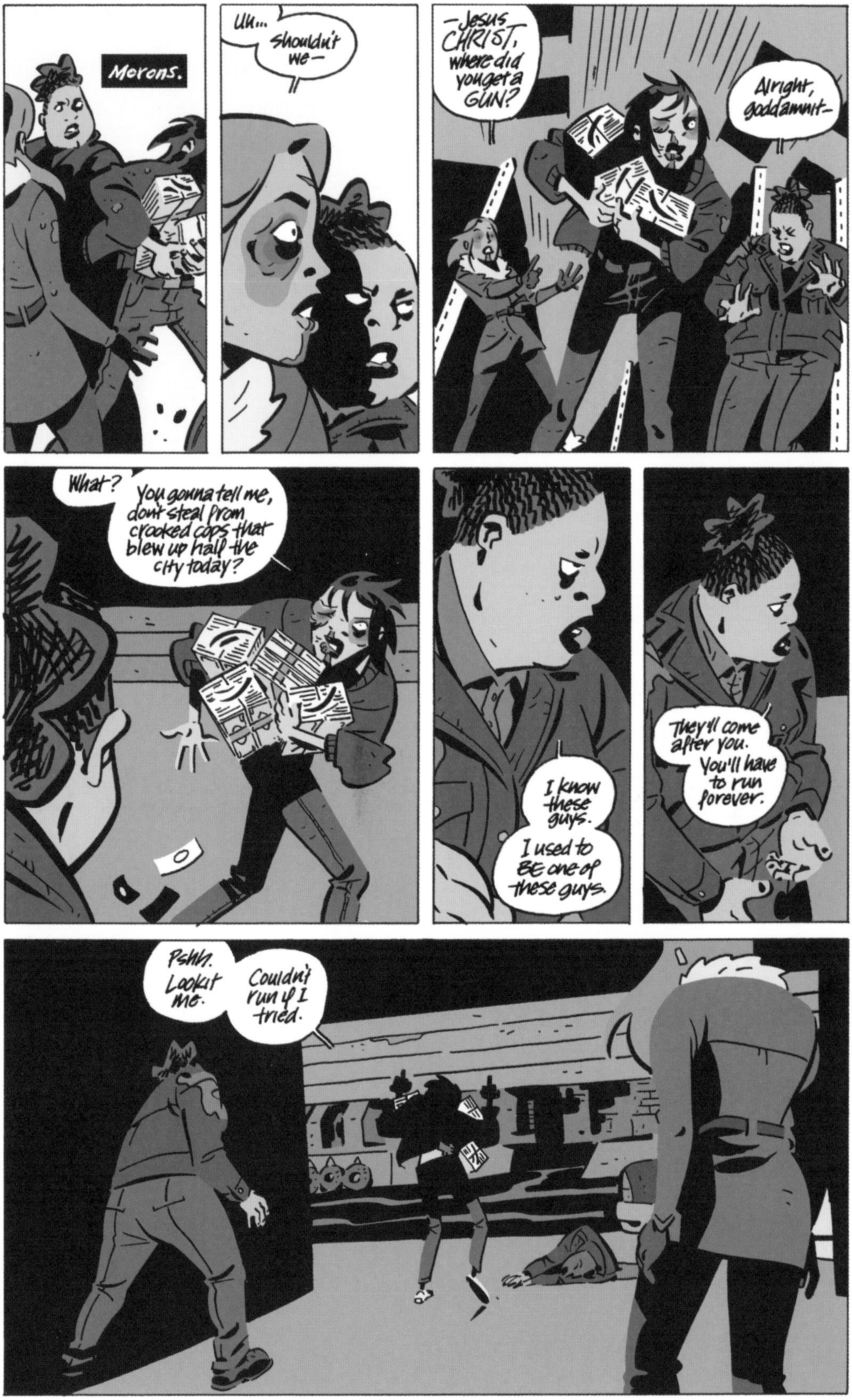
Morons.
Uh... shouldn't we—
—Jesus CHRIST, where did you get a GUN?
Alright, goddamnit—
What?
You gonna tell me, don't steal from crooked cops that blew up half the city today?
I know these guys.
I used to BE one of these guys.
They'll come after you.
You'll have to run forever.
Pshh. Lookit me.
Couldn't run if I tried.

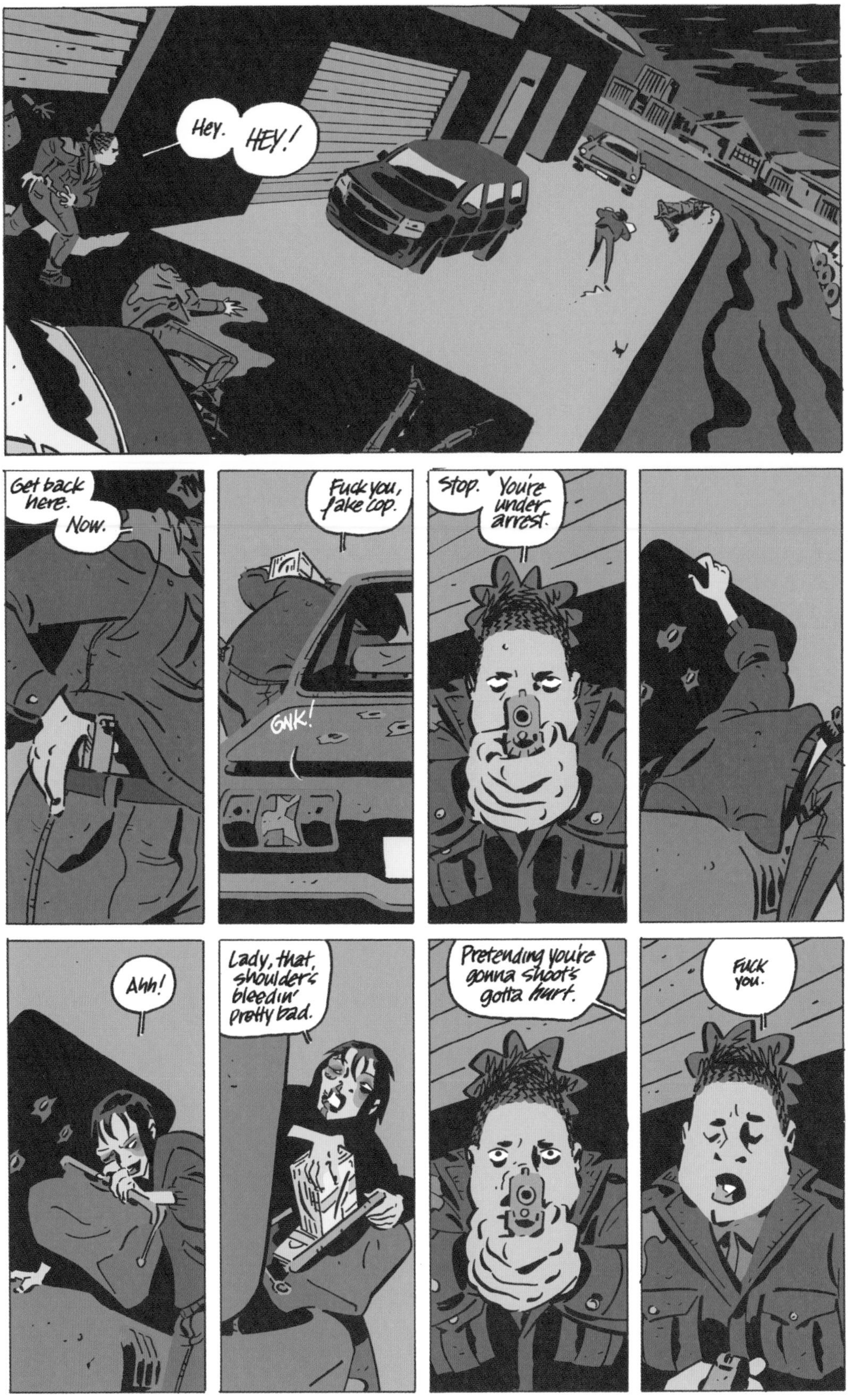
Hey. HEY!
Get back here.
Now.
Fuck you, fake cop.
GNK!
Stop. You're under arrest.
Ahh!
Lady, that shoulder's bleedin' pretty bad.
Pretending you're gonna shoot's gotta hurt.
Fuck you.

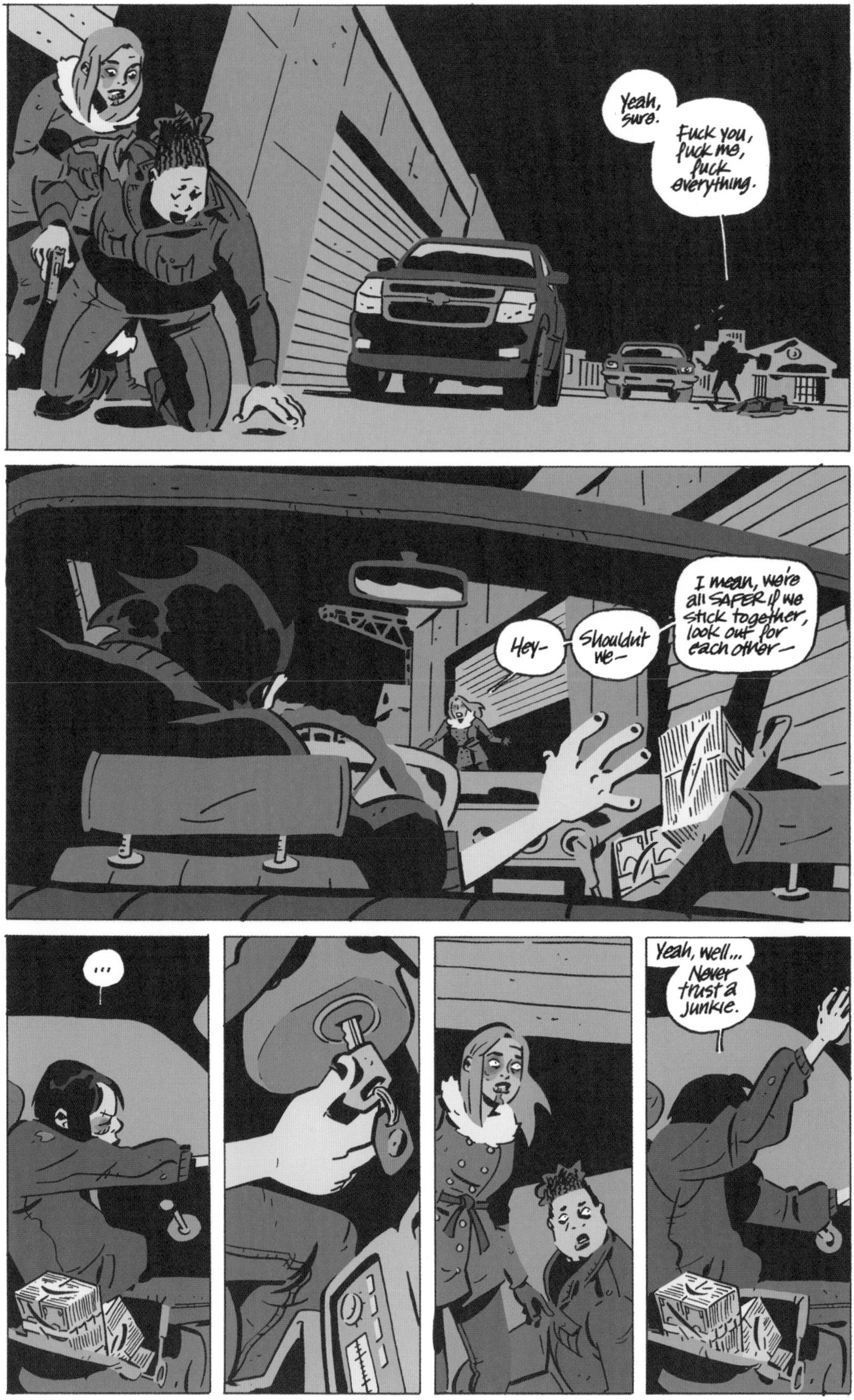
Yeah, sure.
Fuck you, fuck me, fuck everything.
Hey-
Shouldn't we-
I mean, we're all SAFER if we stick together, look out for each other-
...
Yeah, well... Never trust a junkie.

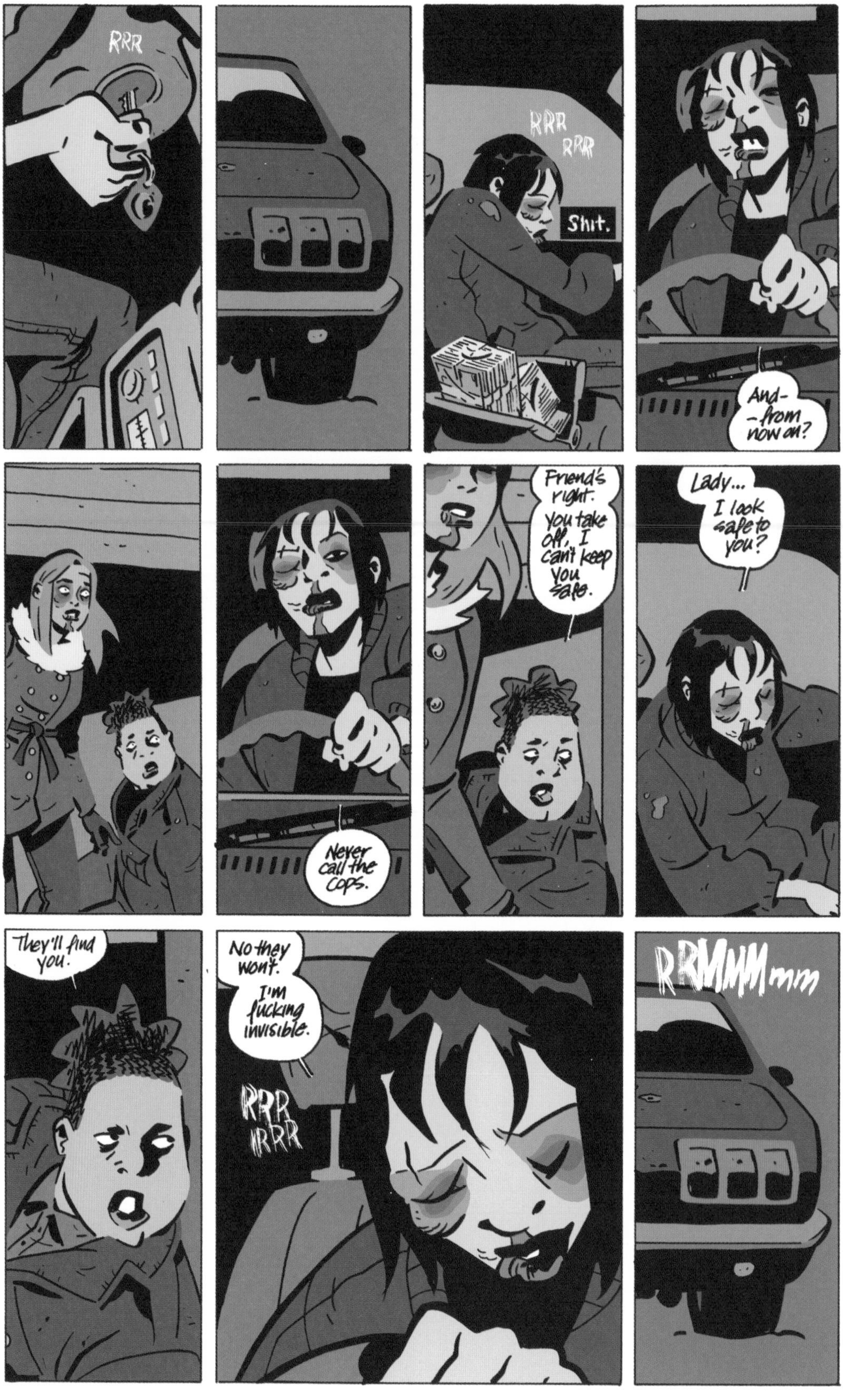
RRR
RRR
RRR
Shit.
And- -from now on?
Never call the cops.
Friend's right. You take off, I can't keep you safe.
Lady... I look safe to you?
They'll find you.
No they won't.
I'm fucking invisible.
RRR
RRR
RRMMMmm

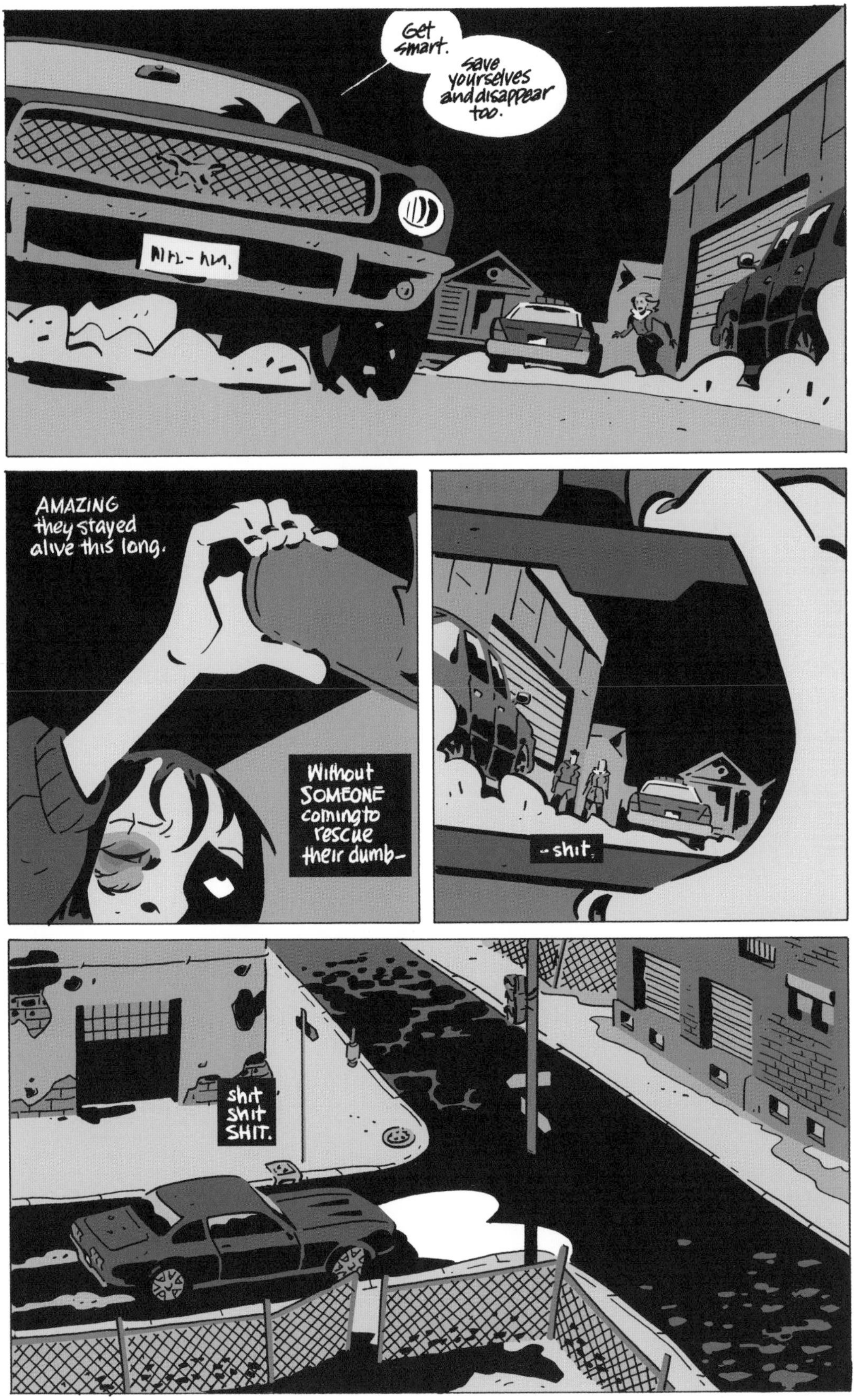
Get smart.
Save yourselves and disappear too.
AMAZING they stayed alive this long.
Without SOMEONE coming to rescue their dumb-
-shit.
shit shit SHIT.

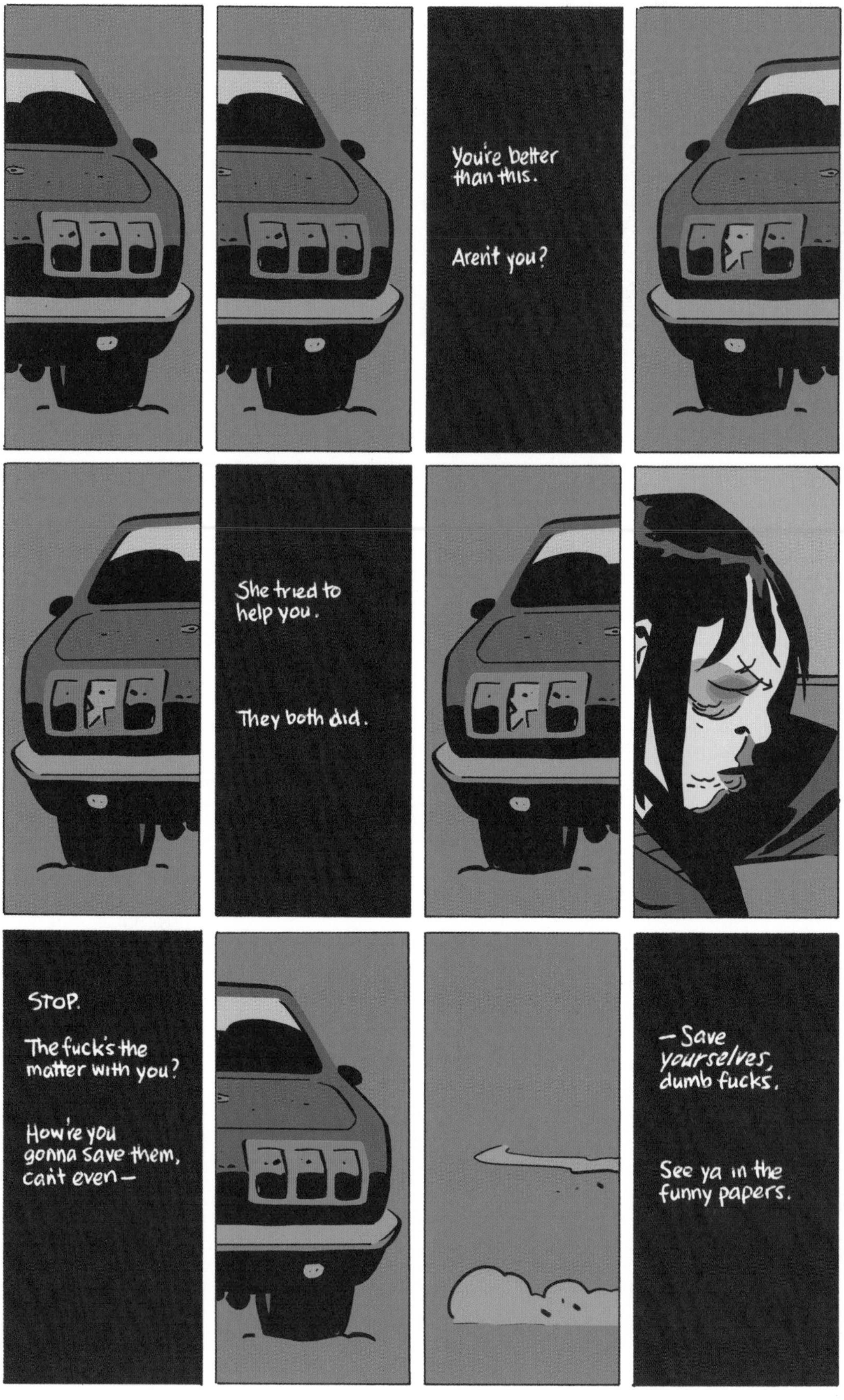
You're better than this.
Aren't you?
She tried to help you.
They both did.
STOP.
The fuck's the matter with you?
How're you gonna save them, can't even—
—Save yourselves, dumb fucks.
See ya in the funny papers.

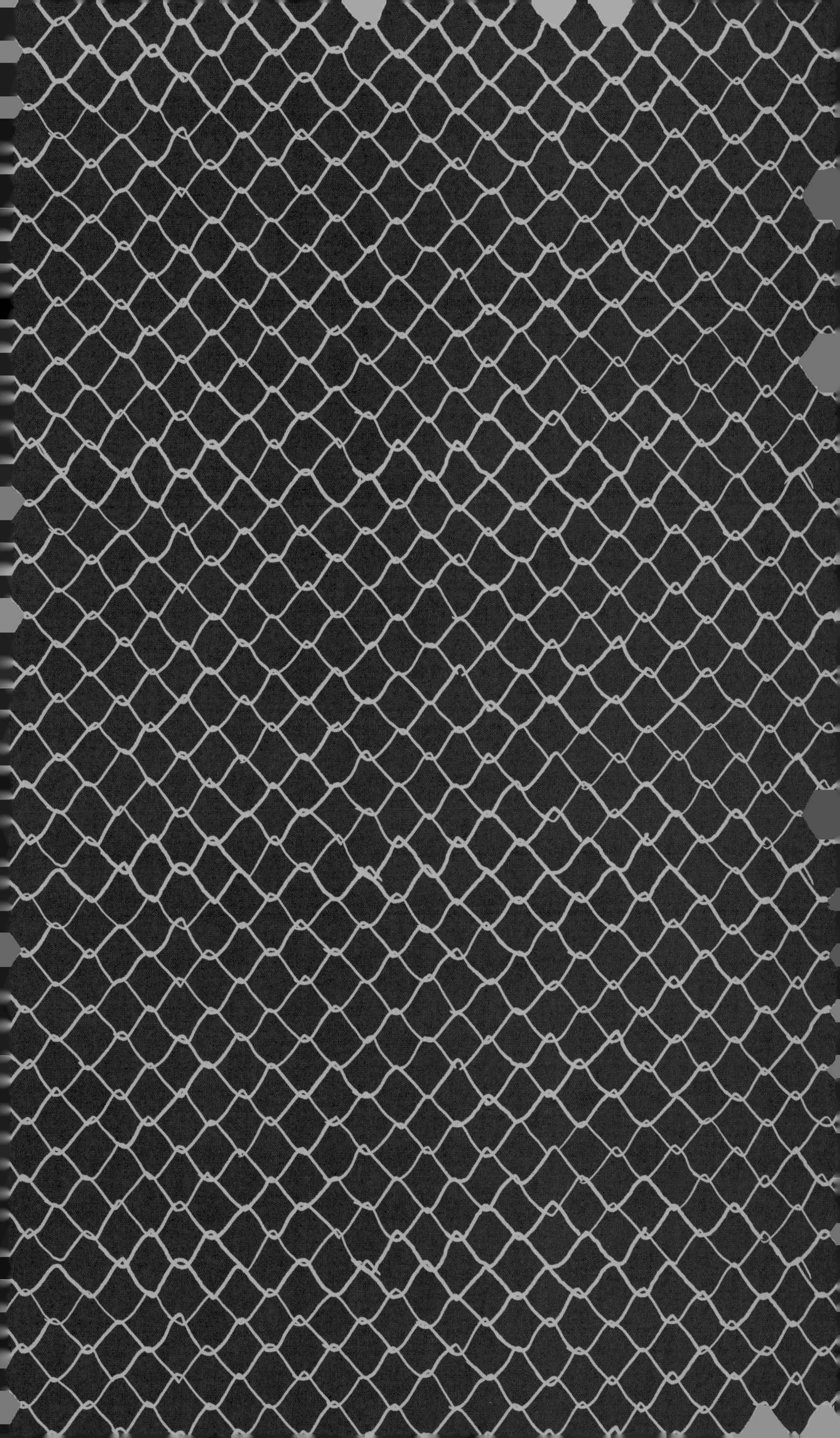

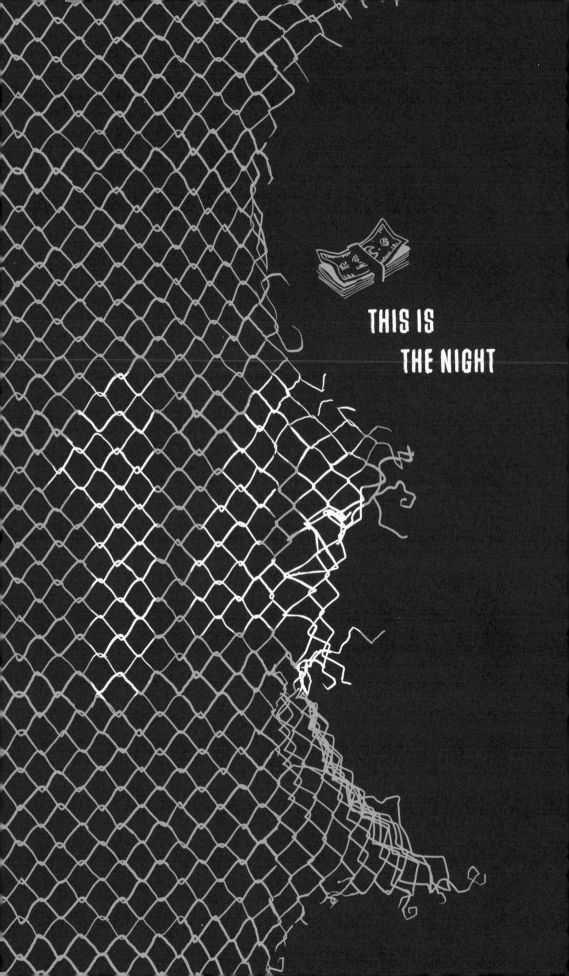

THIS IS
THE NIGHT

FUCK IT.

WHOA WHOA WHOA, HANG ON.

These people.

These women.

I need you to stay where you are.

Just let me fucking THINK for a second—

WAIT, C'MON NOW. LET'S DO WHAT SHE SAYS. I MEAN—

SHE'S A COP.

Why aren't they listening to me?

These women are crazy.

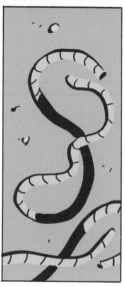

Run, Em.

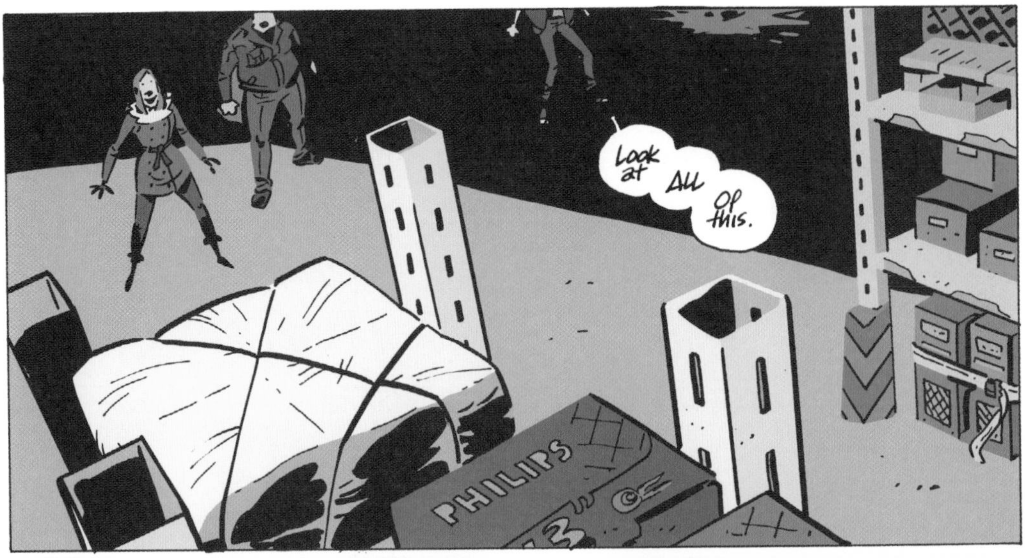
Look at ALL of this.
PHILIPS

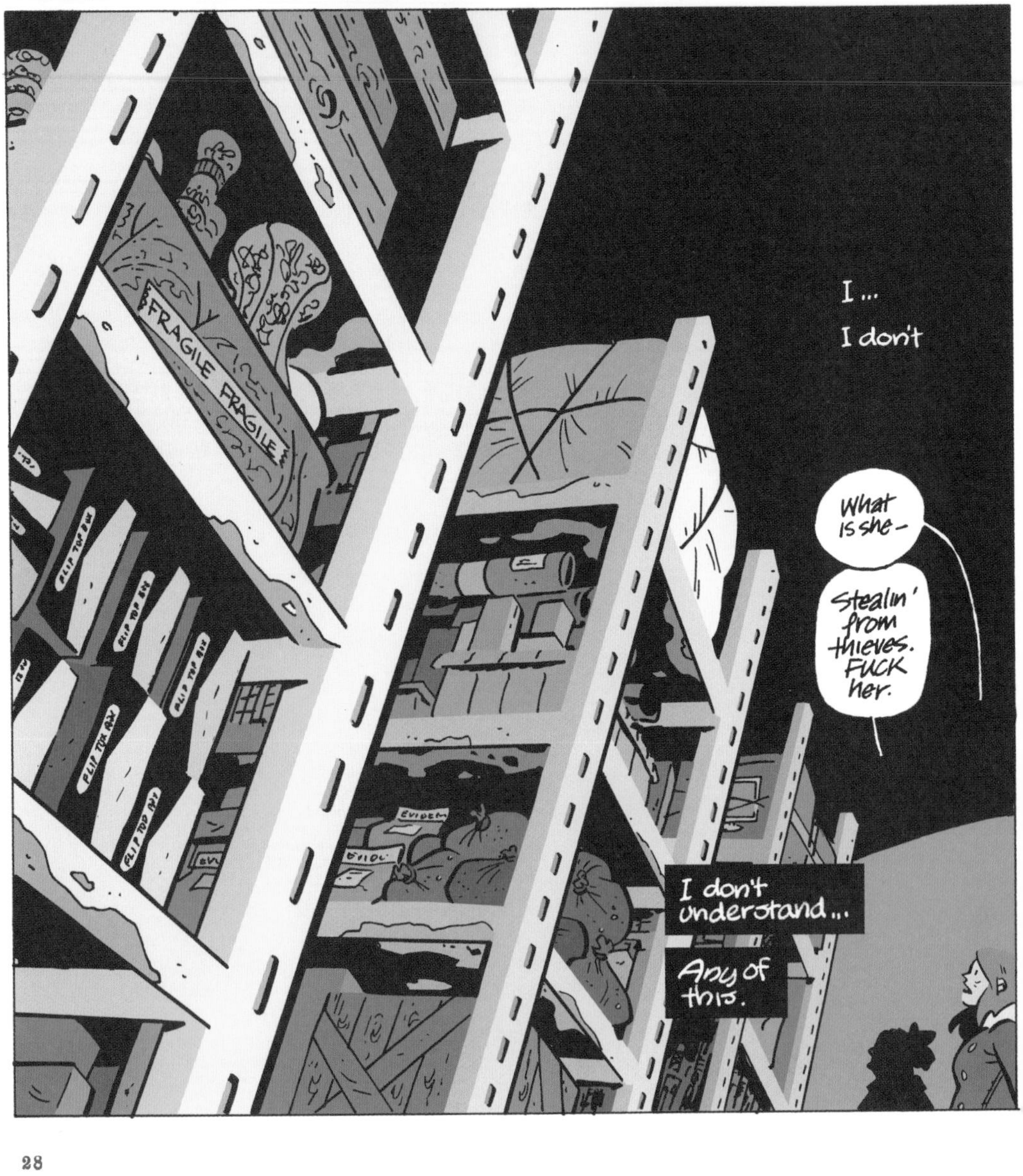
FRAGILE FRAGILE
I...
I don't
What is she-
Stealin' from thieves. FUCK her.
I don't understand...
Any of this.

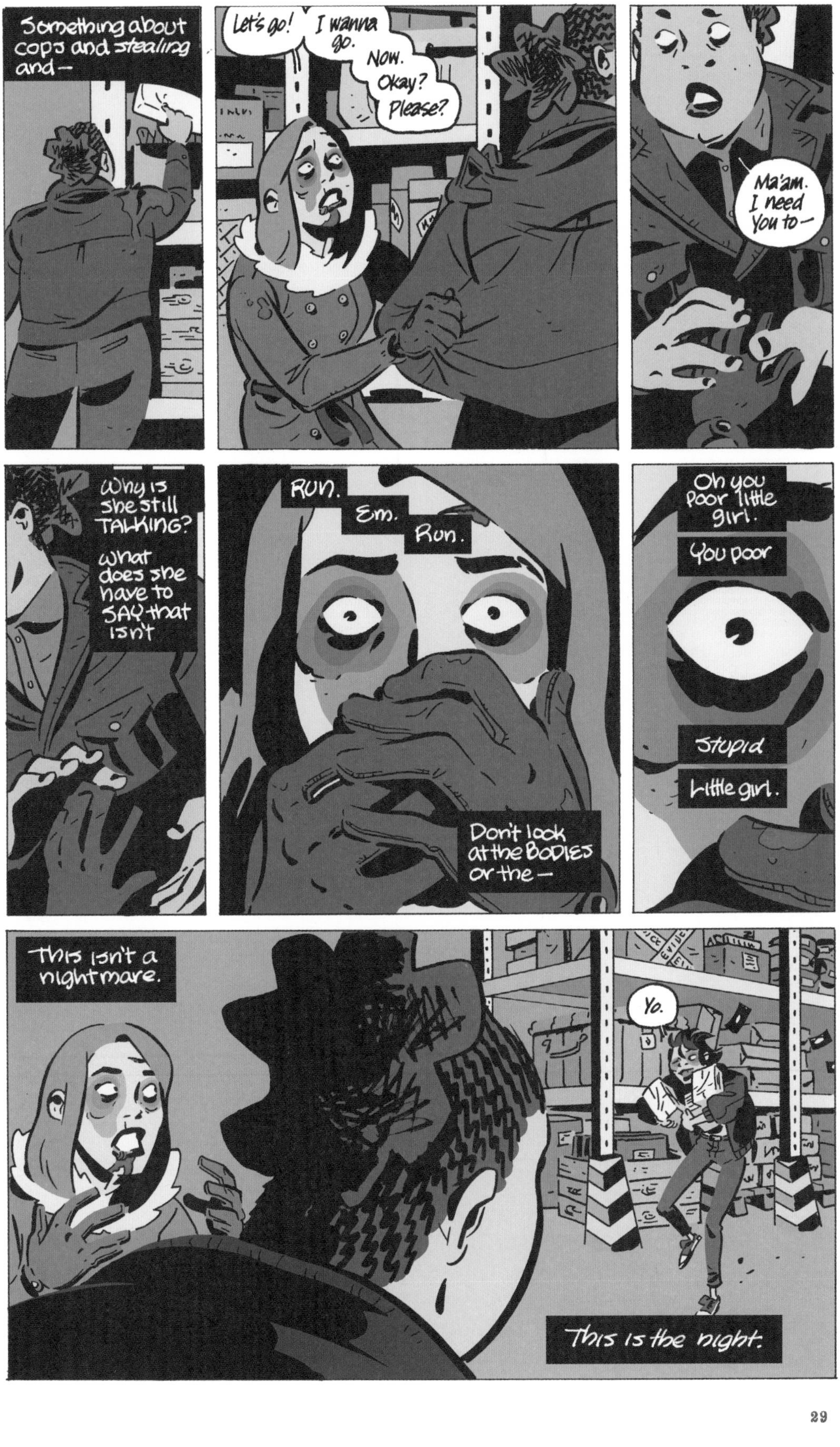
Something about cops and stealing and—
Let's go!
I wanna go.
Now.
Okay?
Please?
Ma'am. I need You to—
Why is she still TALKING?
What does she have to SAY that isn't
RUN.
Em.
Run.
Don't look at the BODIES or the—
Oh you poor little girl.
You poor
Stupid
Little girl.
This isn't a nightmare.
Yo.
This is the night.

And I'm in a playground for monsters

Filled with monstrous things.

I don't belong here.

Jesus.

Why isn't she stopping her?

She's not listening WHY isn't she —

Uh...

Shouldn't we —

—Jesus CHRIST, where did you get a GUN?

Alright, goddammit—

They keep fighting.

And ARGUING and

And and and

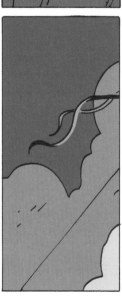

They're not running.

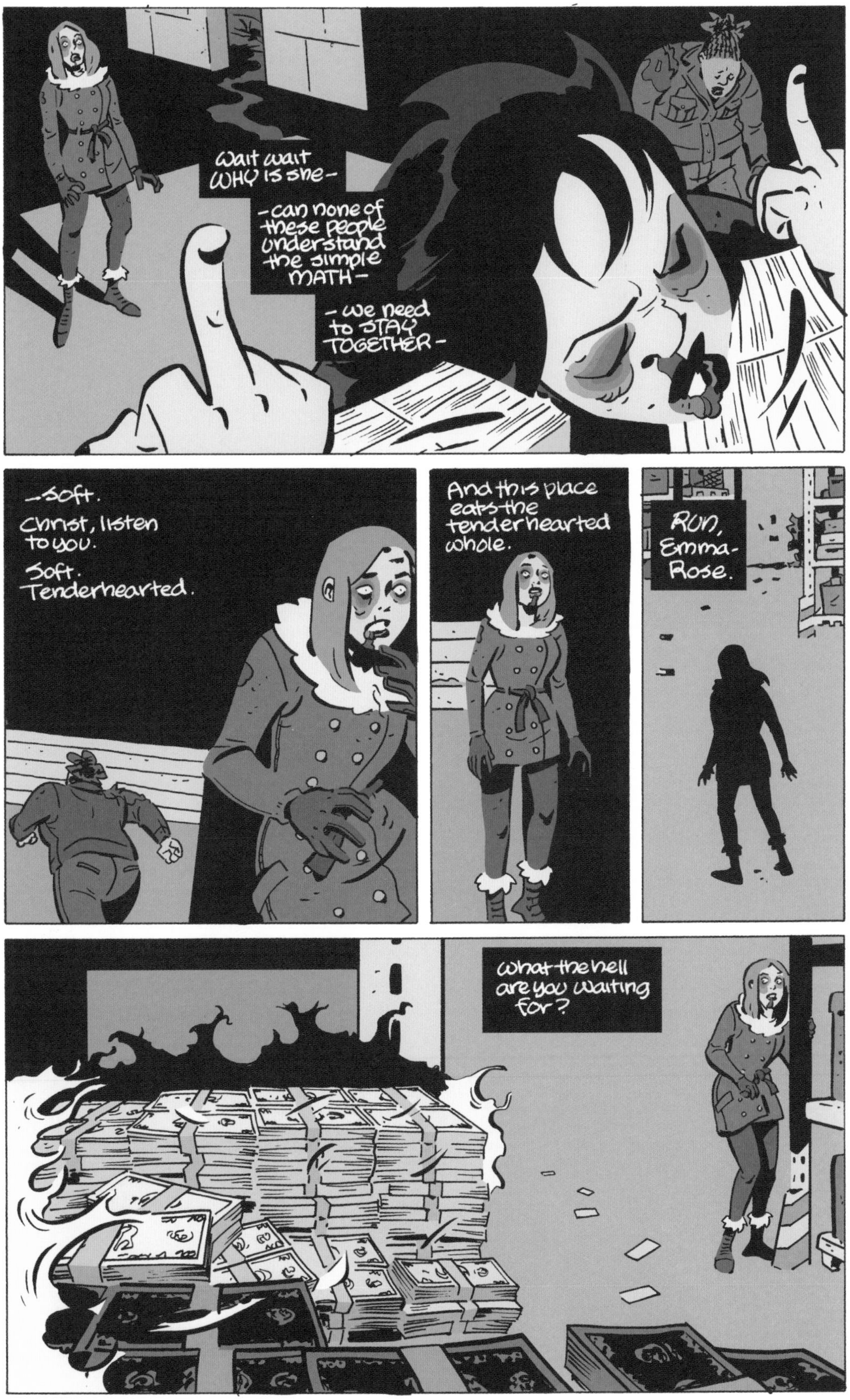
Wait wait WHY is she-
-can none of these people understand the simple MATH-
-we need to STAY TOGETHER-
-soft.
Christ, listen to you.
Soft. Tenderhearted.
And this place eats the tenderhearted whole.
RUN, Emma-Rose.
What the hell are you waiting for?

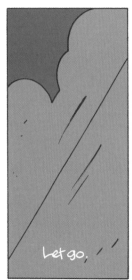

Let go.

Just let go.

Just go towards that door and—

Hey—

Shouldn't we—

I mean, we're all SAFER if we stick together, look out for each other—

She doesn't care.

She makes fun of me and leaves.

why can't you be more like HER?

why can't YOU be like that?

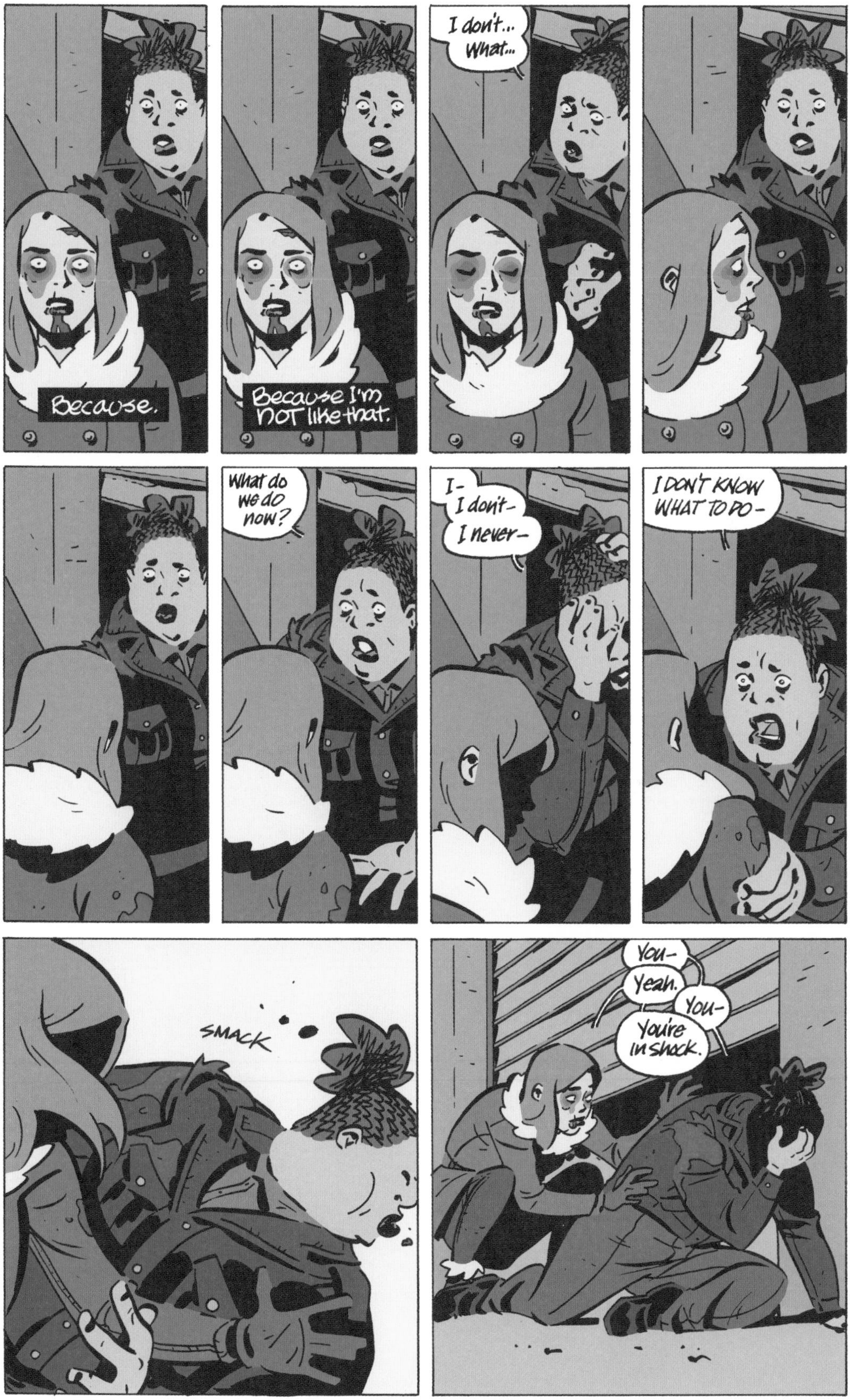
Because.
Because I'm NOT like that.
I don't... What...
What do we do now?
I- I don't- I never-
I DON'T KNOW WHAT TO DO-
SMACK
You-
Yeah.
You-
You're in shock.

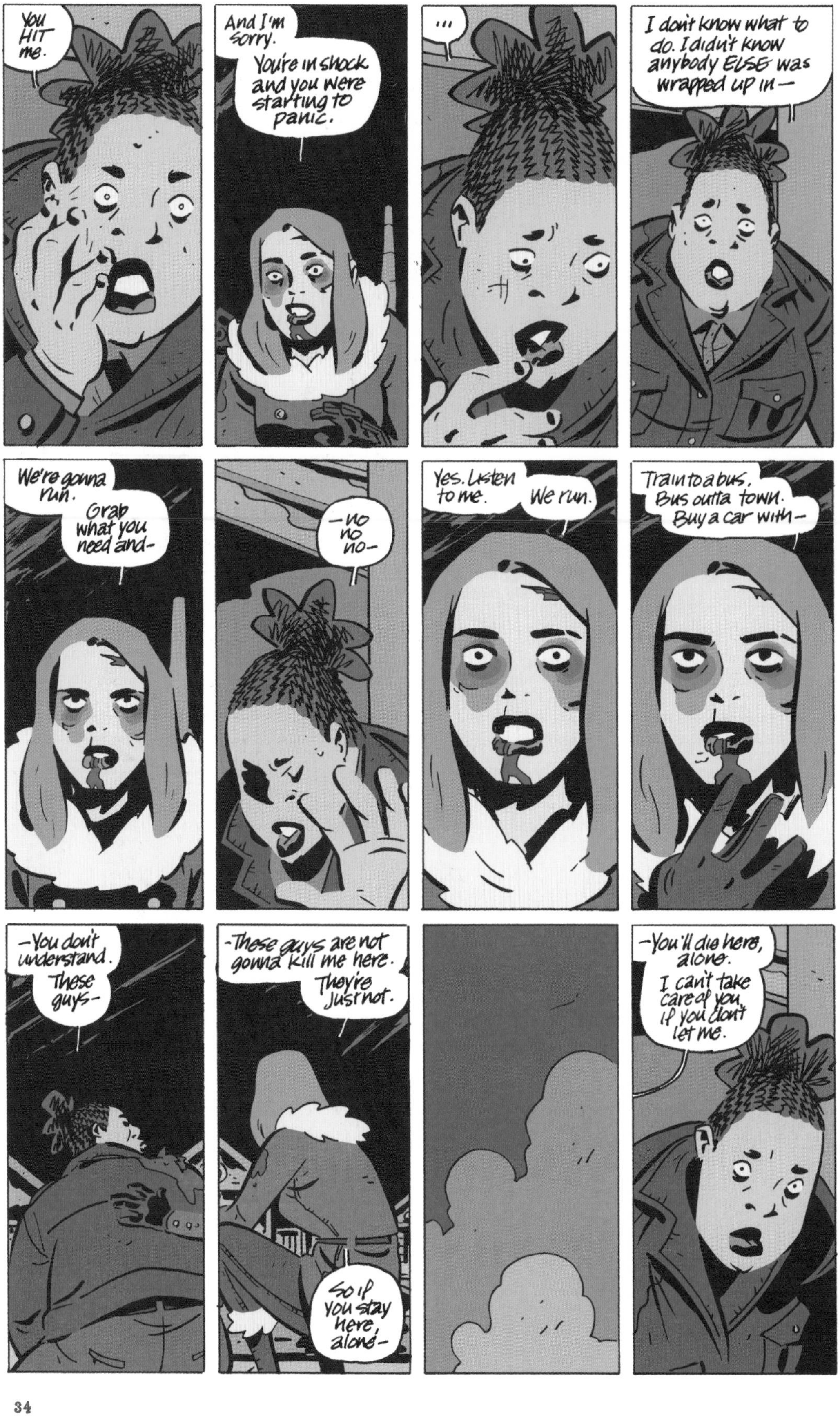
You HIT me.
And I'm sorry.
You're in shock and you were starting to panic.
...
I don't know what to do. I didn't know anybody ELSE was wrapped up in—
We're gonna run.
Grab what you need and-
-no no no-
Yes. Listen to me.
We run.
Train to a bus. Bus outta town. Buy a car with-
-You don't understand.
These guys-
-These guys are not gonna kill me here.
They're just not.
So if you stay here, alone-
-You'll die here, alone.
I can't take care of you if you don't let me.

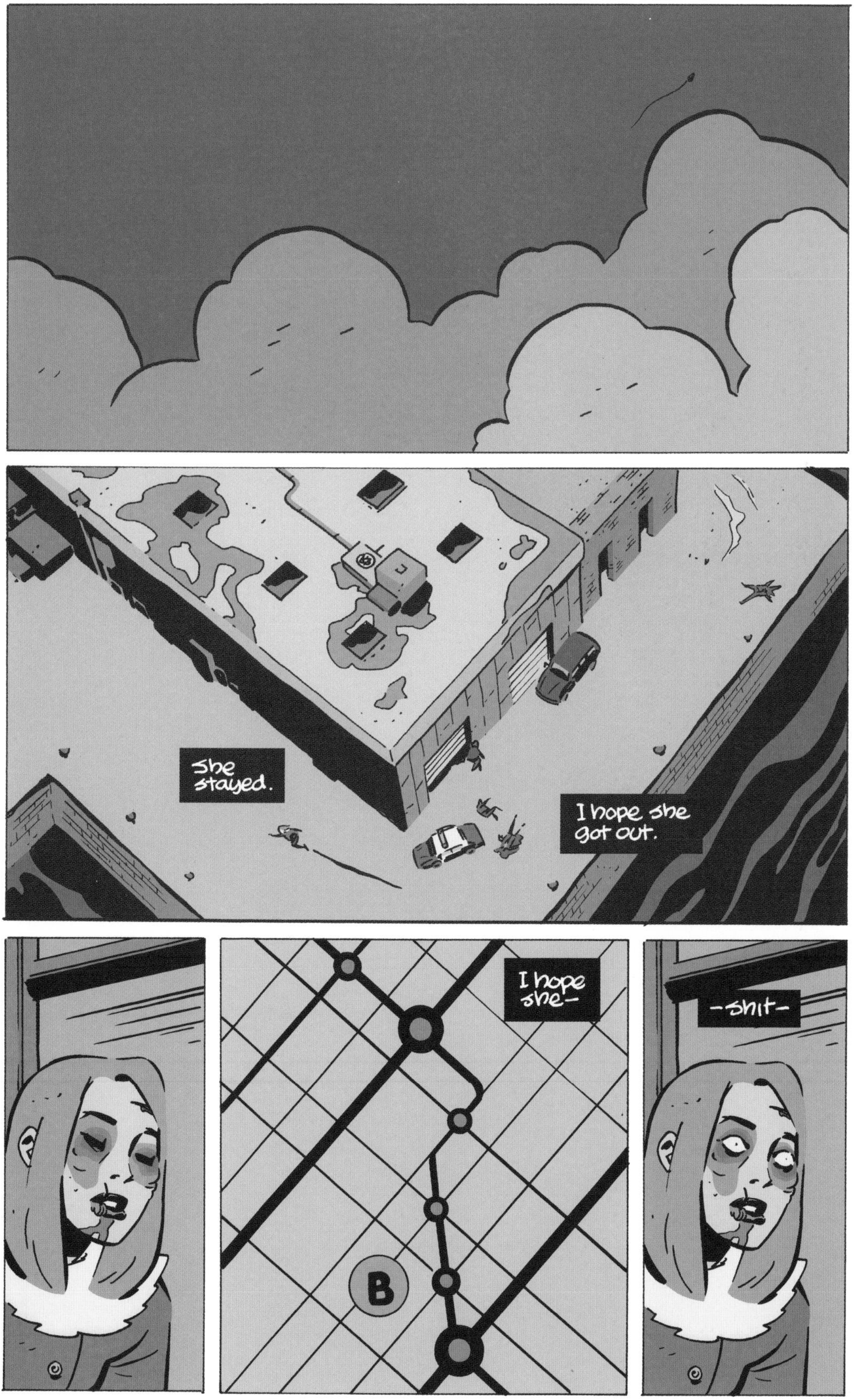
She stayed.
I hope she got out.
I hope she—
—shit—

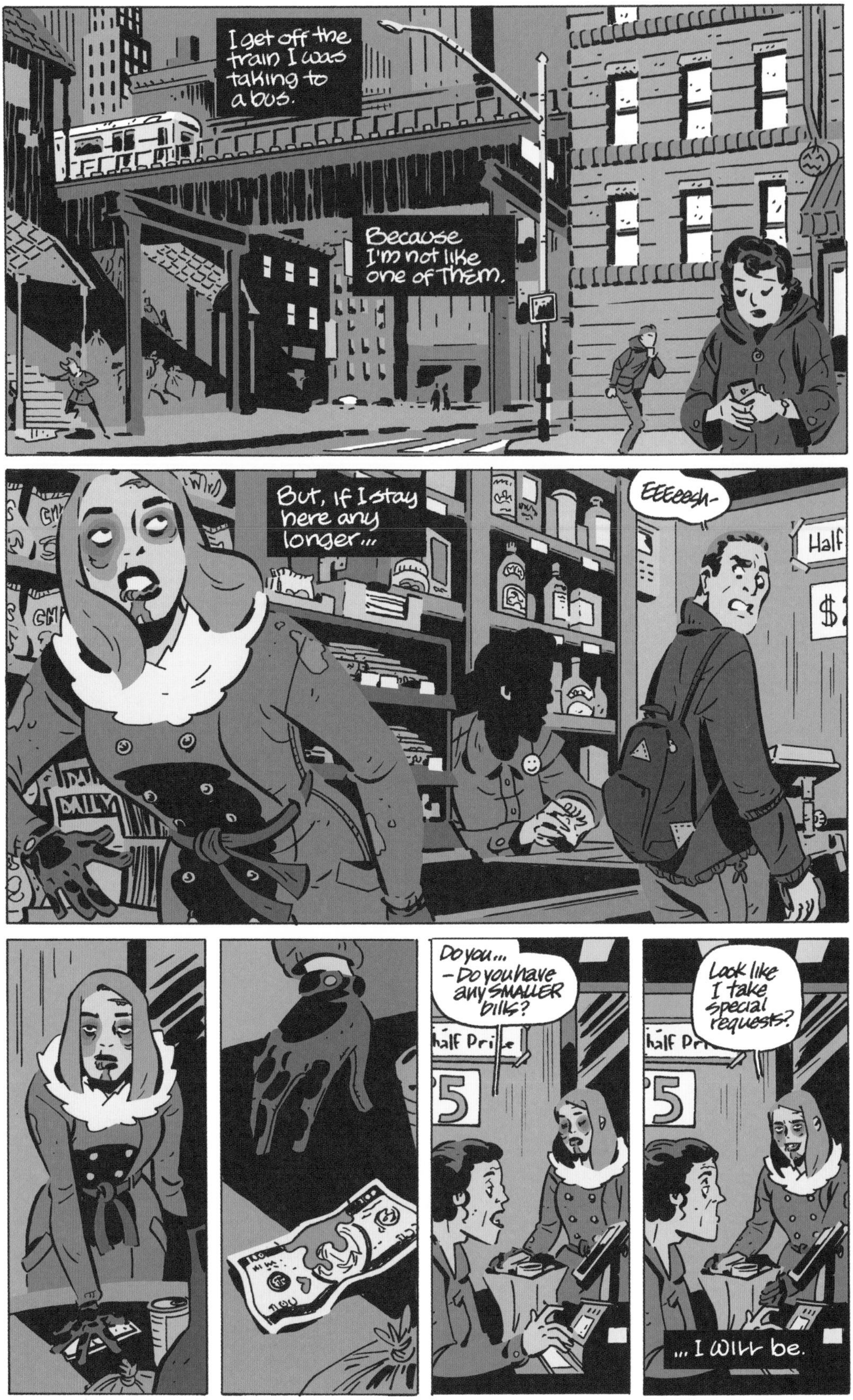
I get off the train I was taking to a bus.
Because I'm not like one of THEM.
But, if I stay here any longer...
EEEeeesh-
Half
Do you... -Do you have any SMALLER bills?
Half Price
Look like I take special requests?
Half Price
...I will be.

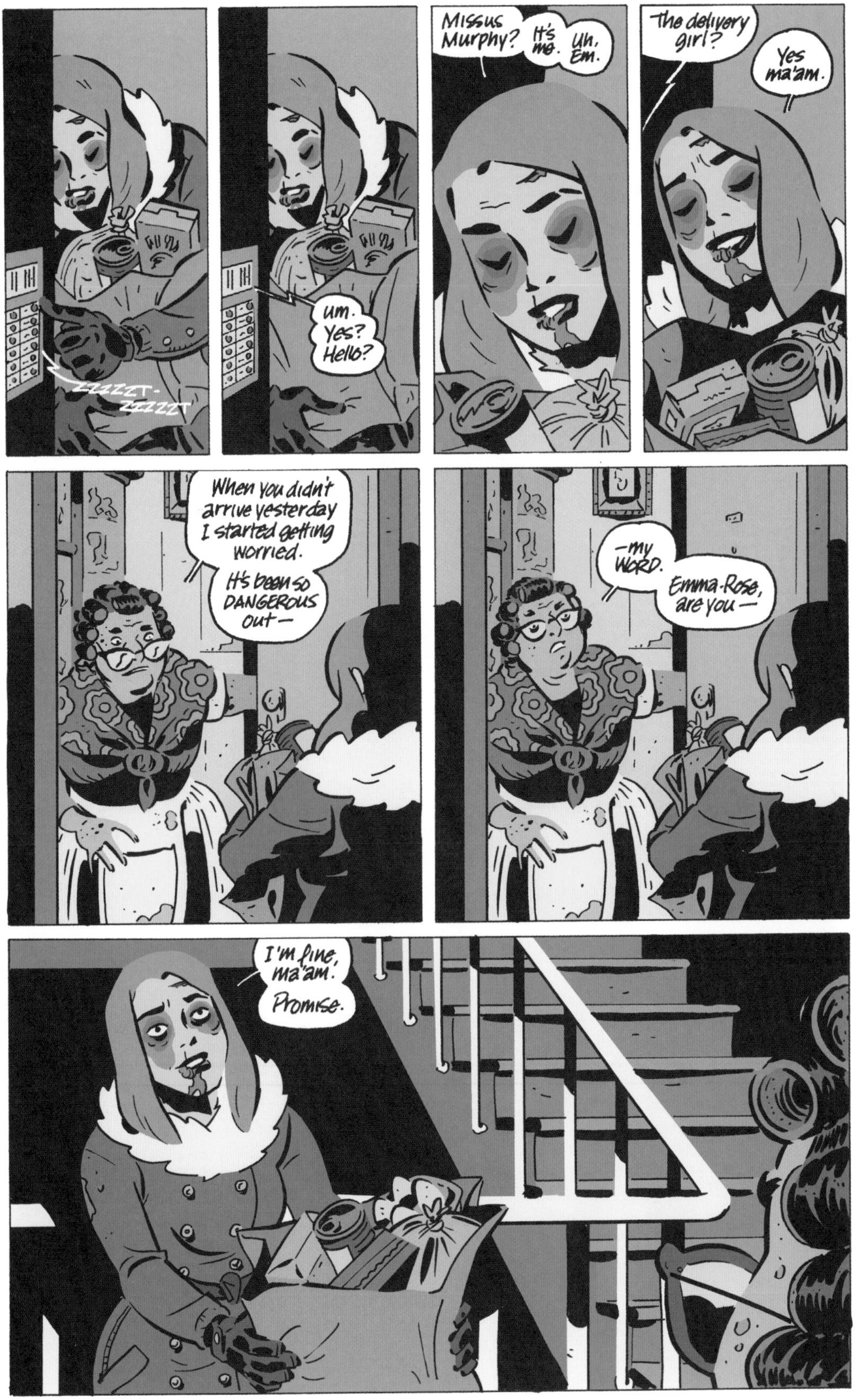
ZZZZZT-ZZZZZT
Um. Yes? Hello?
Missus Murphy?
It's me.
Uh, Em.
The delivery girl?
Yes ma'am.
When you didn't arrive yesterday I started getting worried.
It's been so DANGEROUS out—
—my WORD.
Emma-Rose, are you—
I'm fine, ma'am.
Promise.

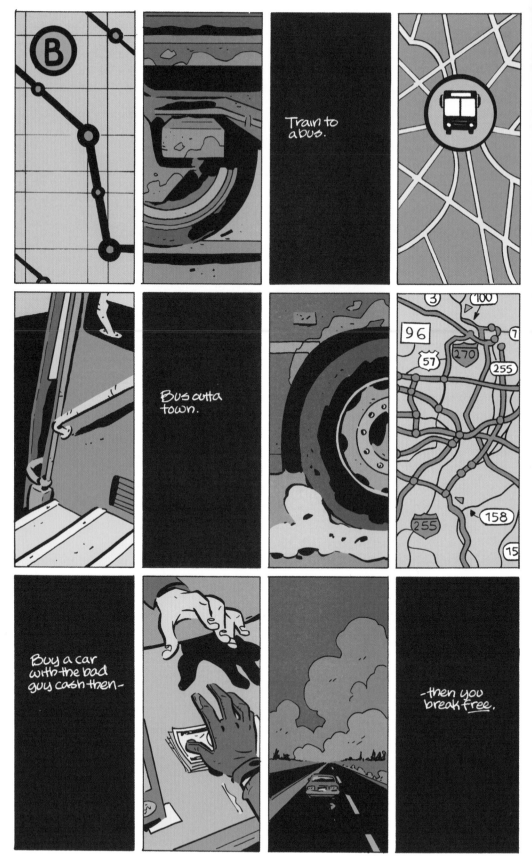

Train to
a bus.

Bus outta
town.

Buy a car
with the bad
guy cash then—

—then you
break free.

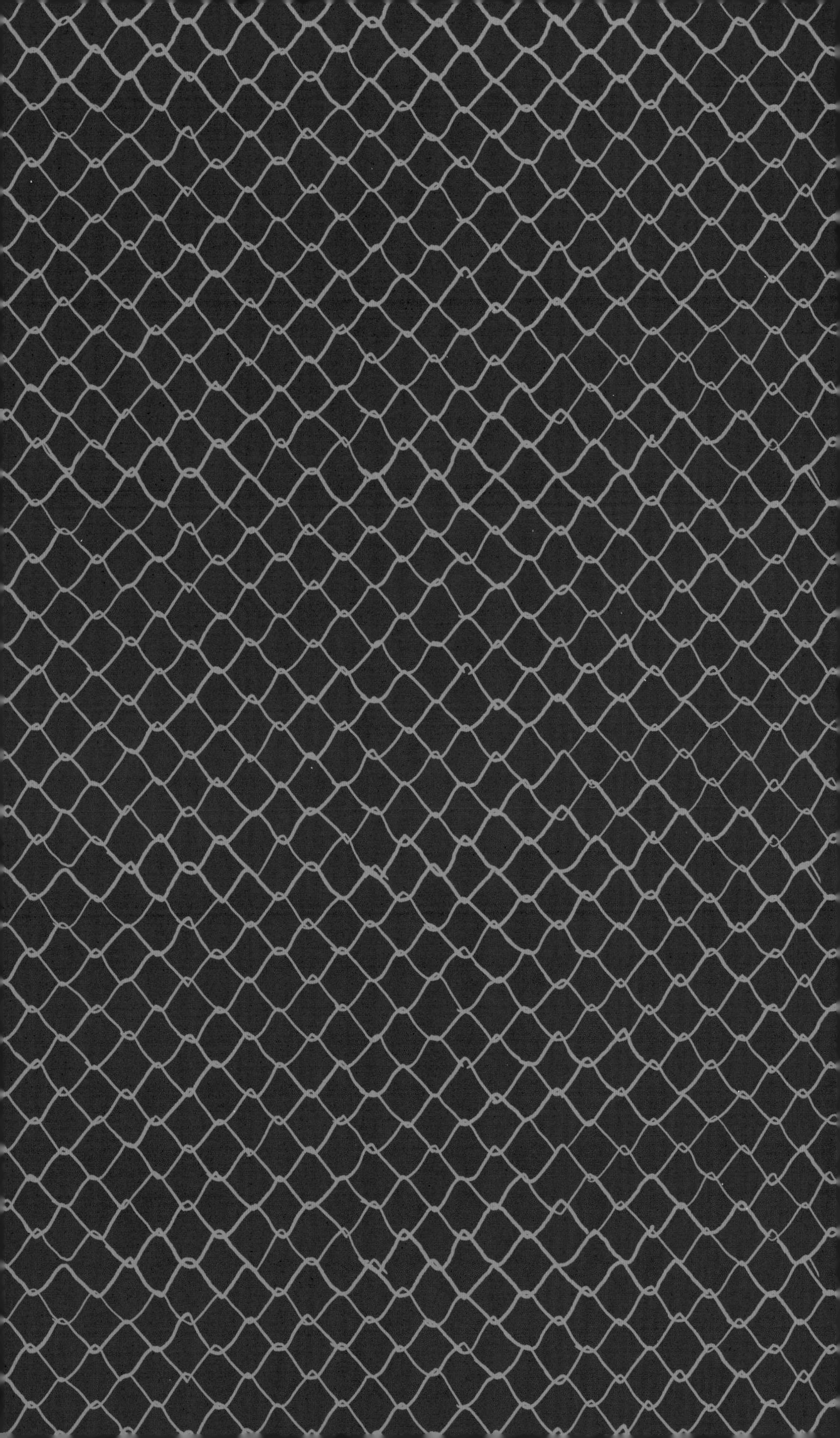

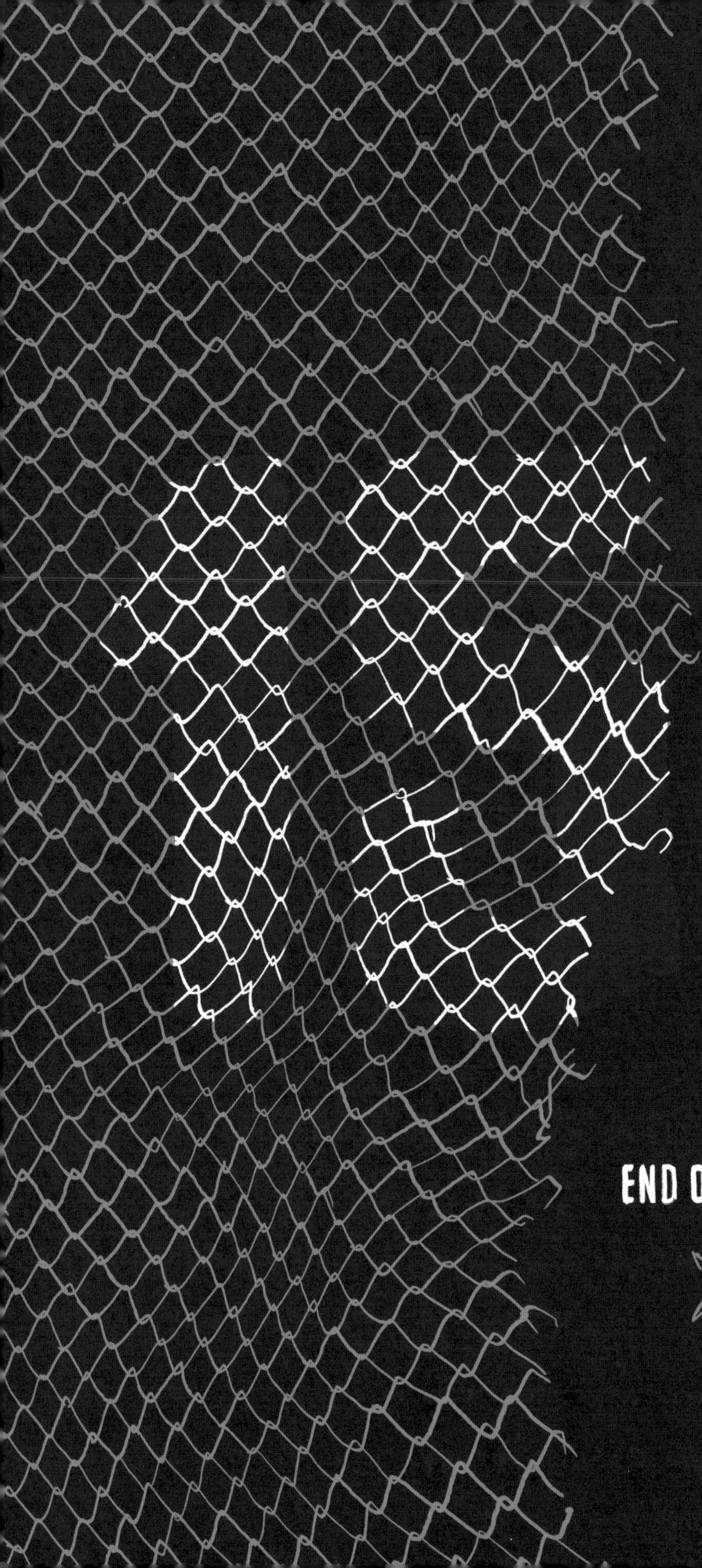

END OF WATCH

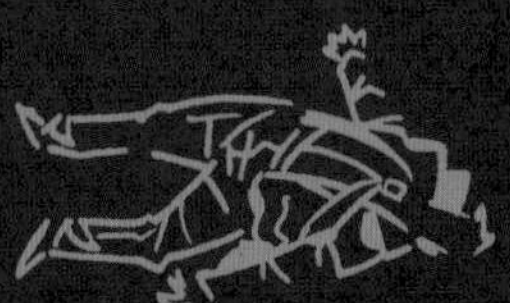

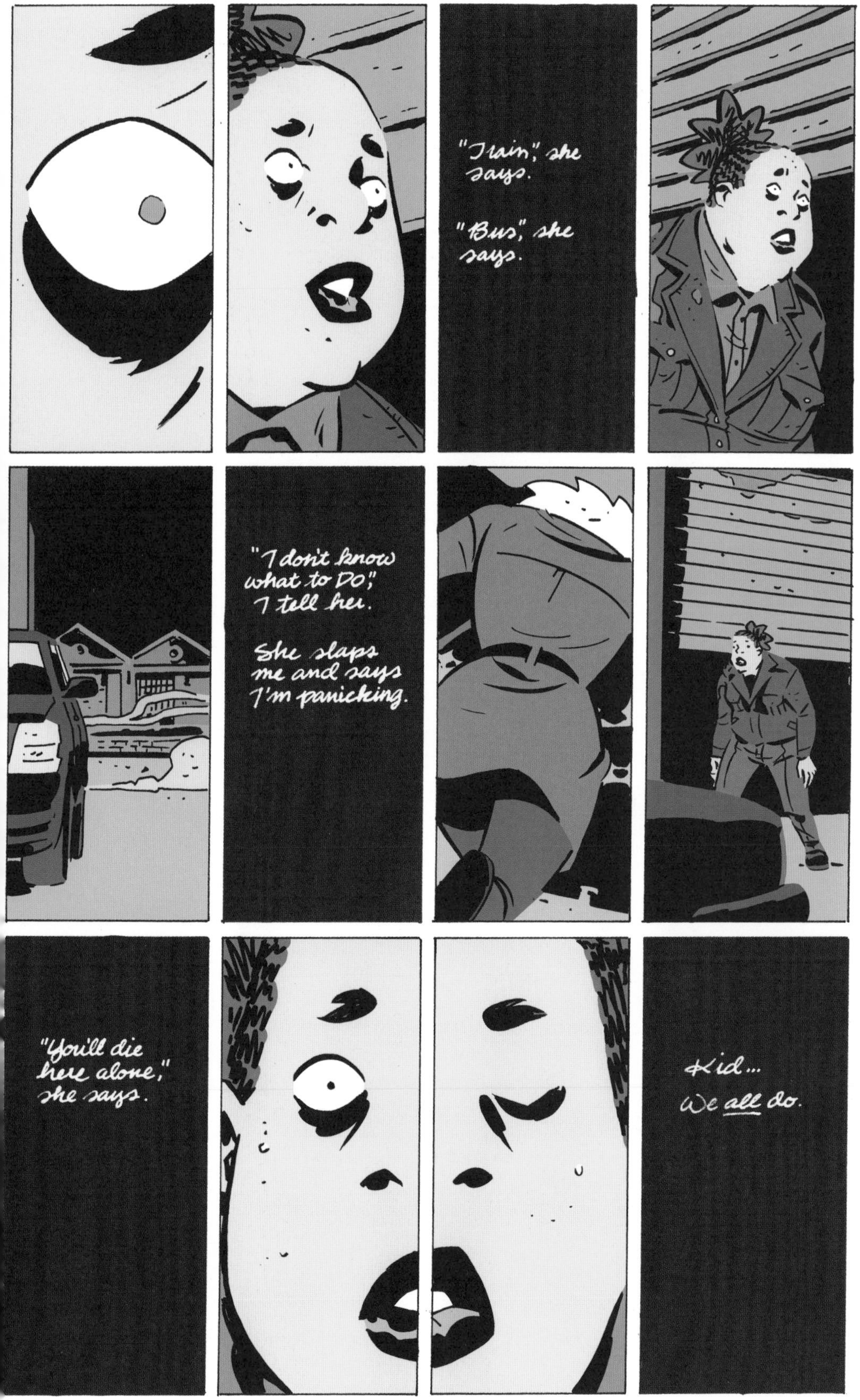
"Train," she says.
"Bus," she says.
"I don't know what to DO," I tell her.
She slaps me and says I'm panicking.
"You'll die here alone," she says.
Kid...
We all do.

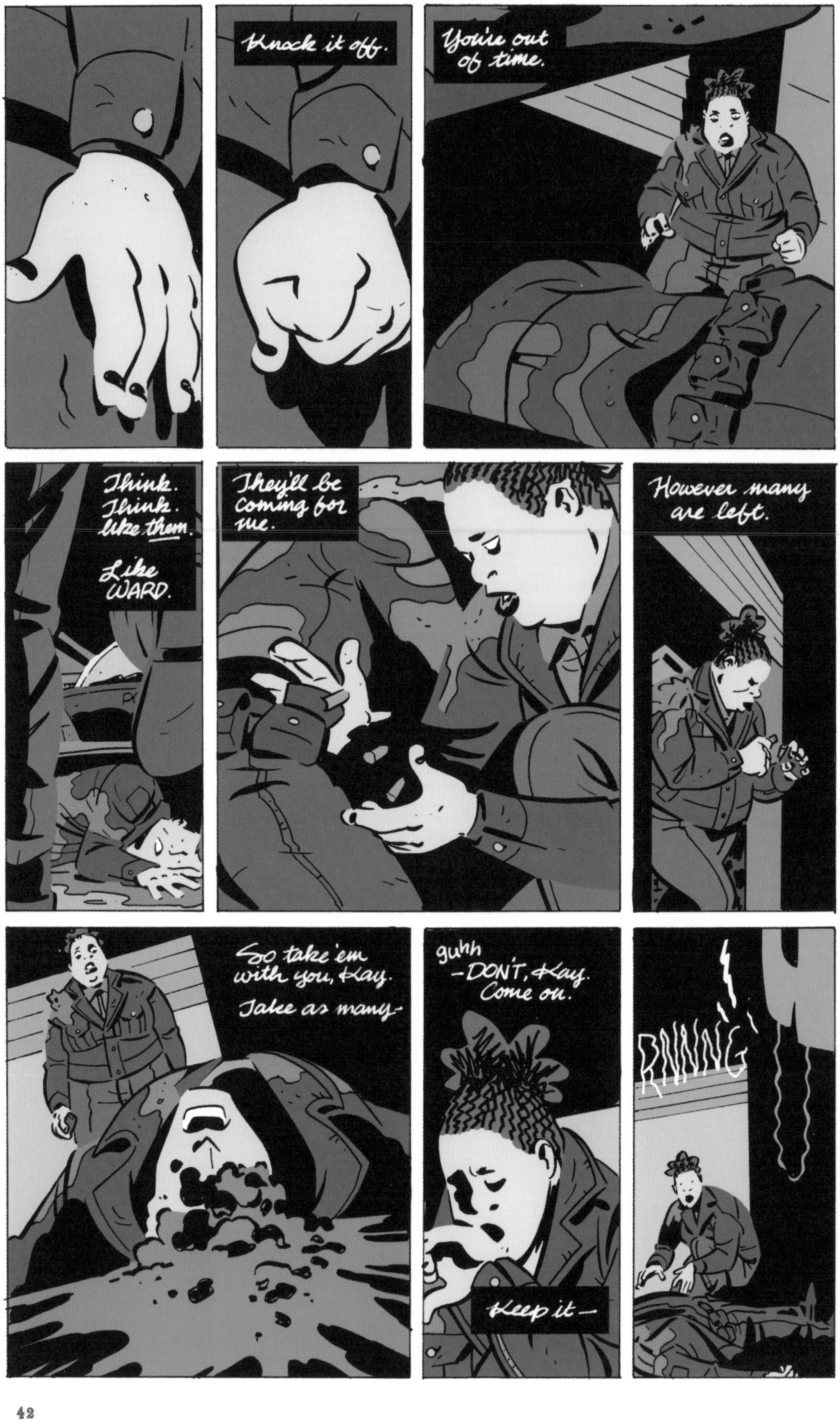
Knock it off.
You're out of time.
Think. Think. Like them.
Like WARD.
They'll be coming for me.
However many are left.
So take 'em with you, Kay.
Take as many-
guhh
-DON'T, Kay. Come on.
Keep it-
RNNNG

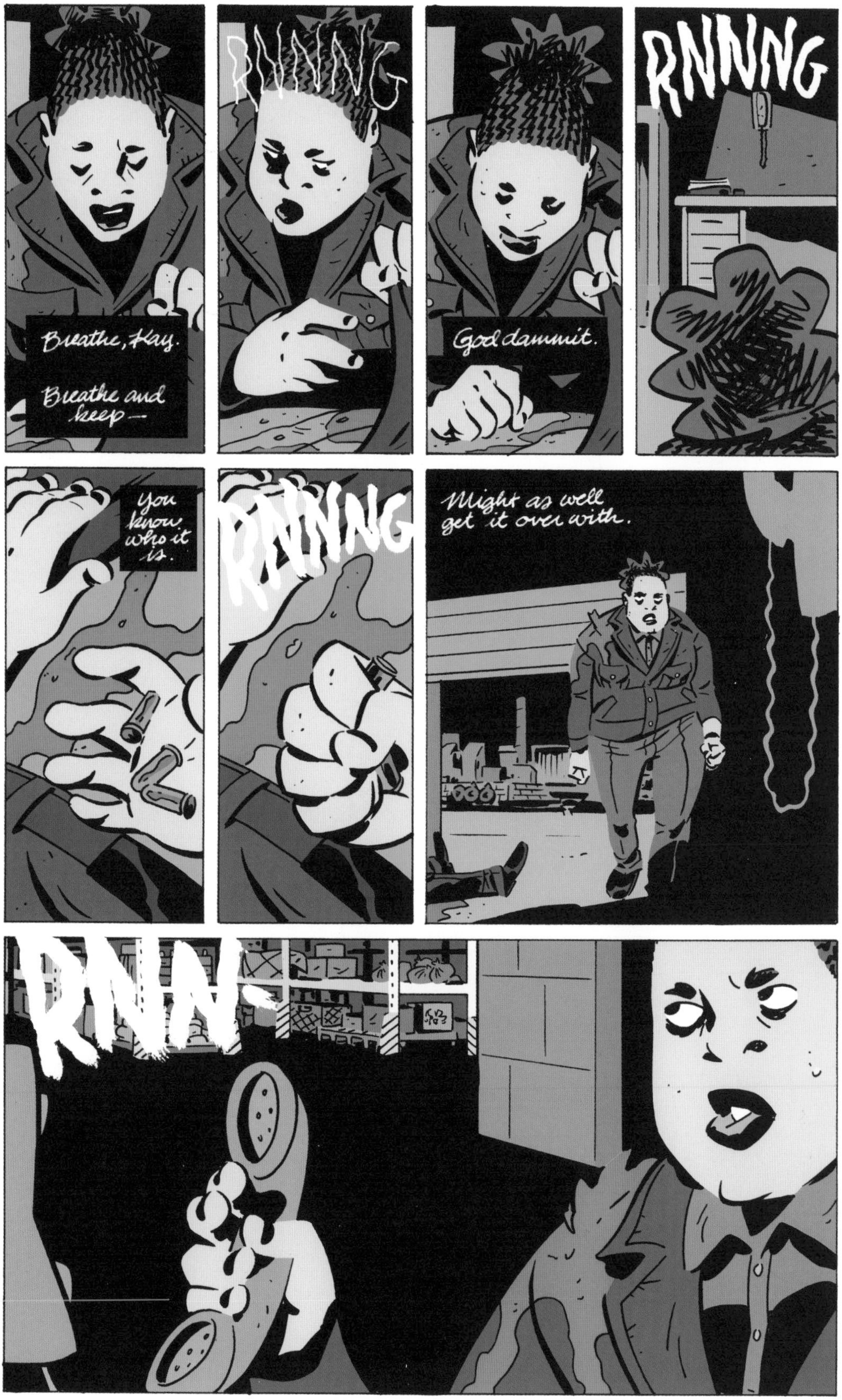
Breathe, Kay.
Breathe and keep—
RNNNG
God dammit.
RNNNG
You know who it is.
RNNNG
Might as well get it over with.
RNN-

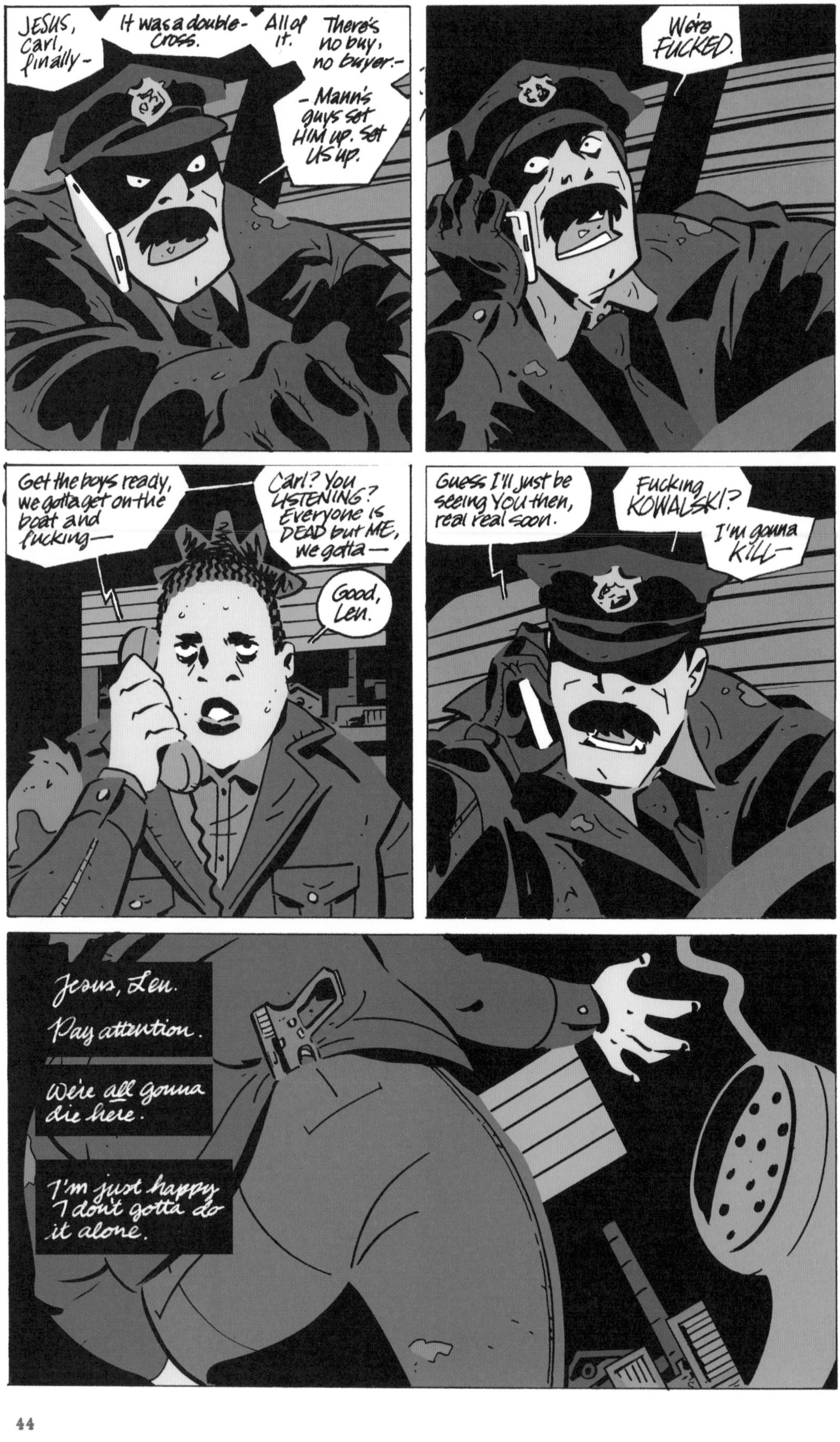
JESUS, Carl, finally -
It was a double-cross.
All of it.
There's no buy, no buyer.-
- Mann's guys set HIM up. Set US up.
We're FUCKED.
Get the boys ready, we gotta get on the boat and fucking—
Carl? You LISTENING? Everyone is DEAD but ME, we gotta—
Good, Len.
Guess I'll just be seeing you then, real real soon.
Fucking KOWALSKI?
I'm gonna KILL—
Jesus, Len.
Pay attention.
We're all gonna die here.
I'm just happy I don't gotta do it alone.

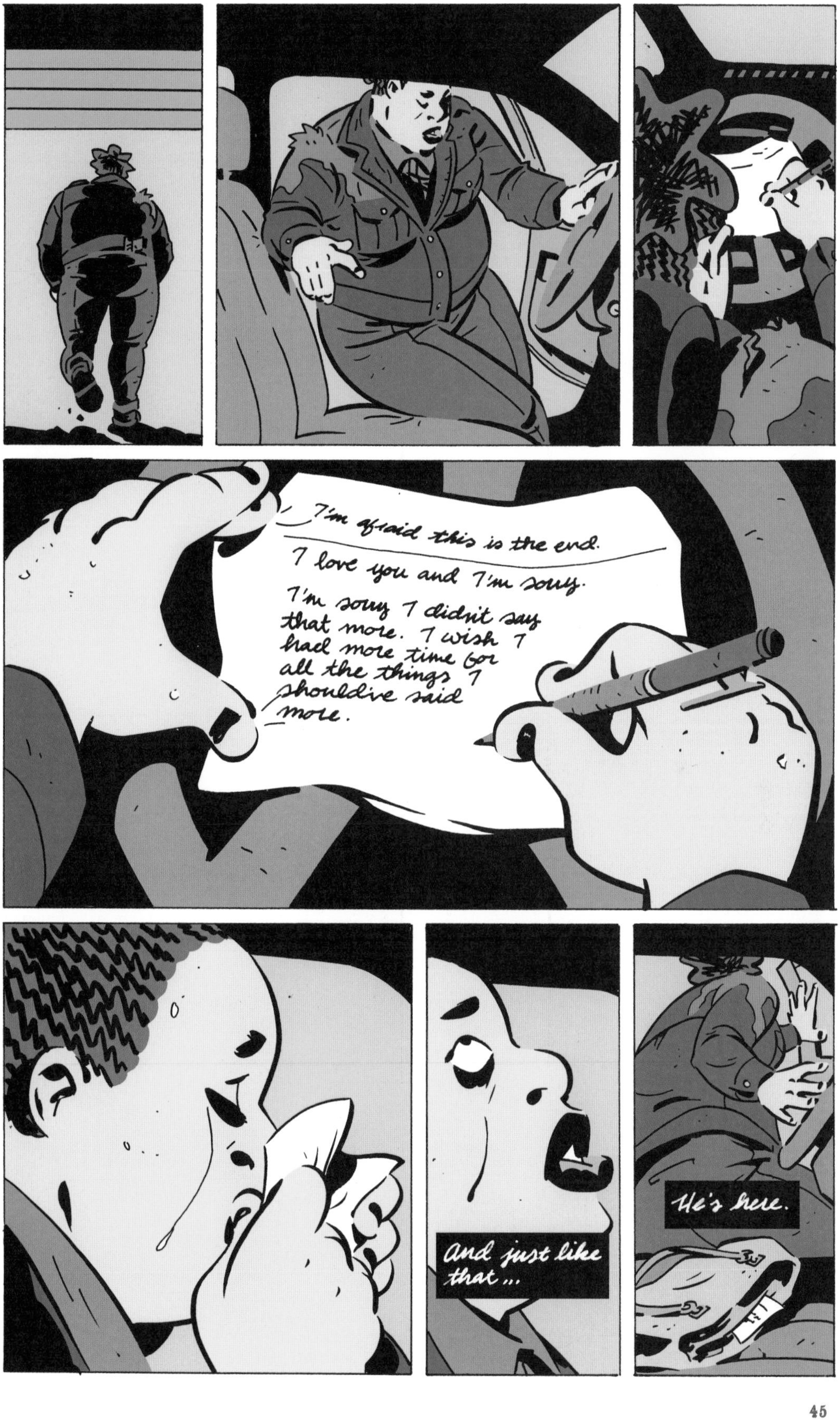
I'm afraid this is the end.
I love you and I'm sorry.
I'm sorry I didn't say that more. I wish I had more time for all the things I should've said more.
And just like that...
He's here.

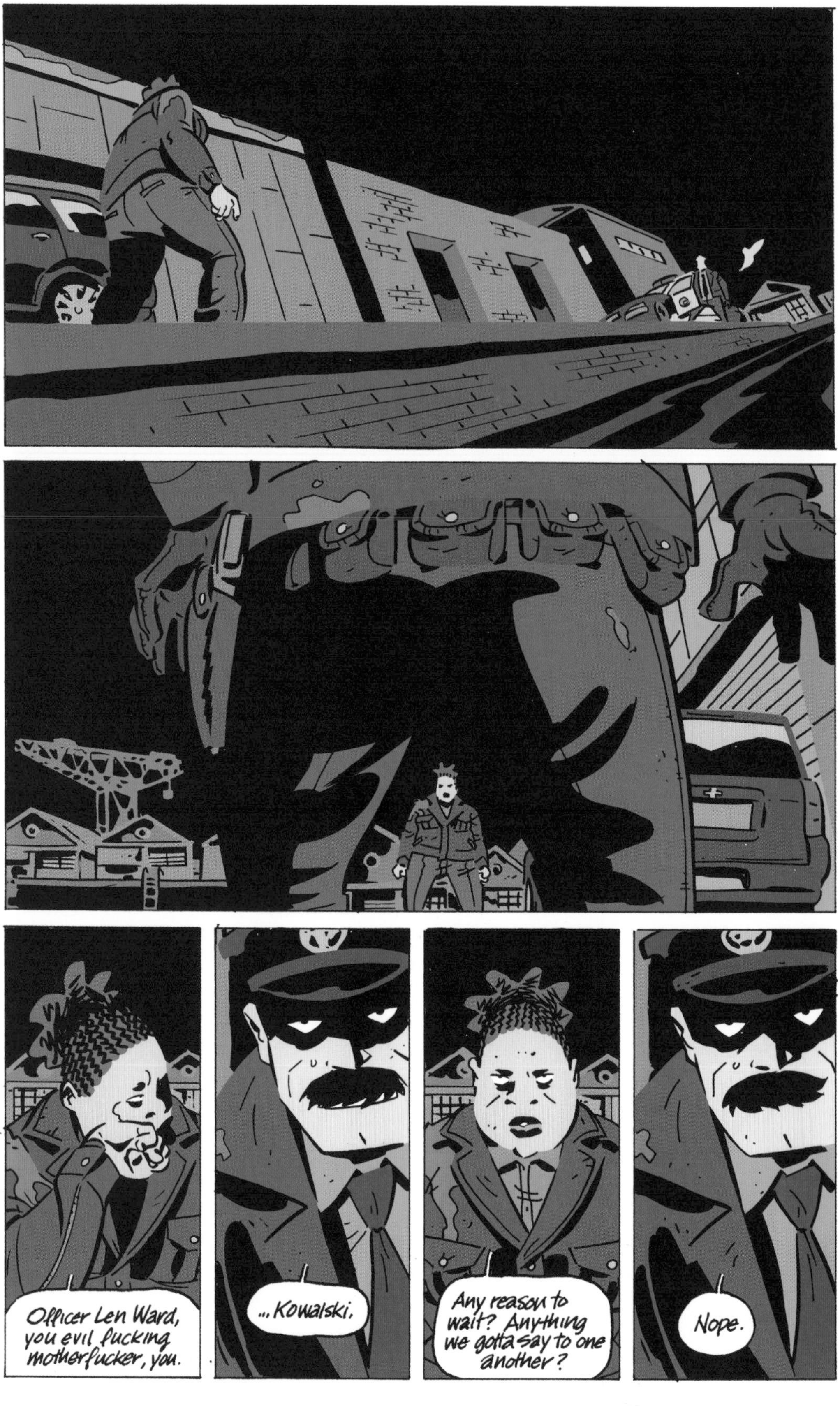

Officer Len Ward, you evil fucking motherfucker, you.
...Kowalski.
Any reason to wait? Anything we gotta say to one another?
Nope.

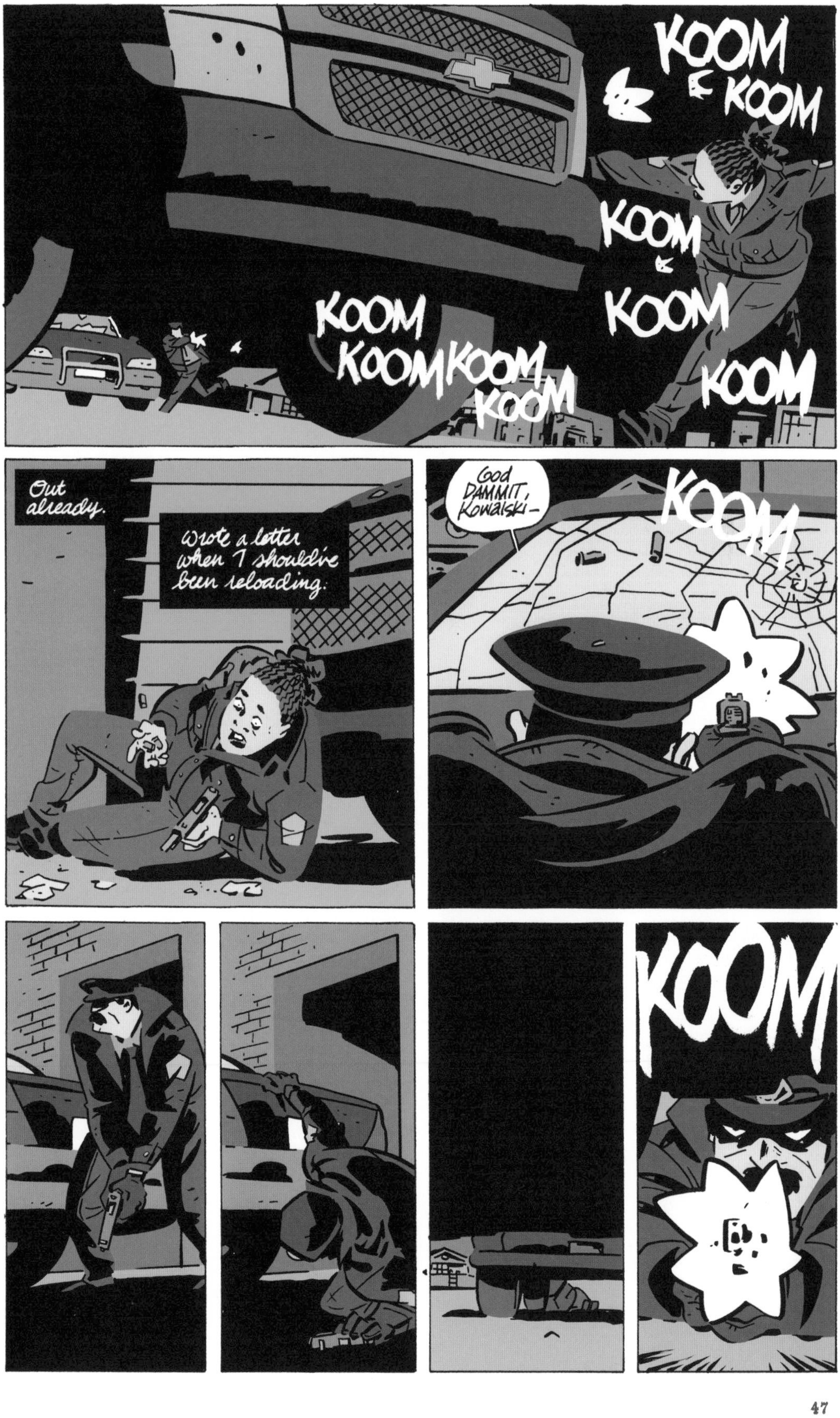
KOOM
KOOM
KOOM
KOOM
KOOM
KOOM
KOOM
KOOM
KOOM
Out already.
Wrote a letter when I should've been reloading.
God DAMMIT, Kowalski—
KOOM
KOOM

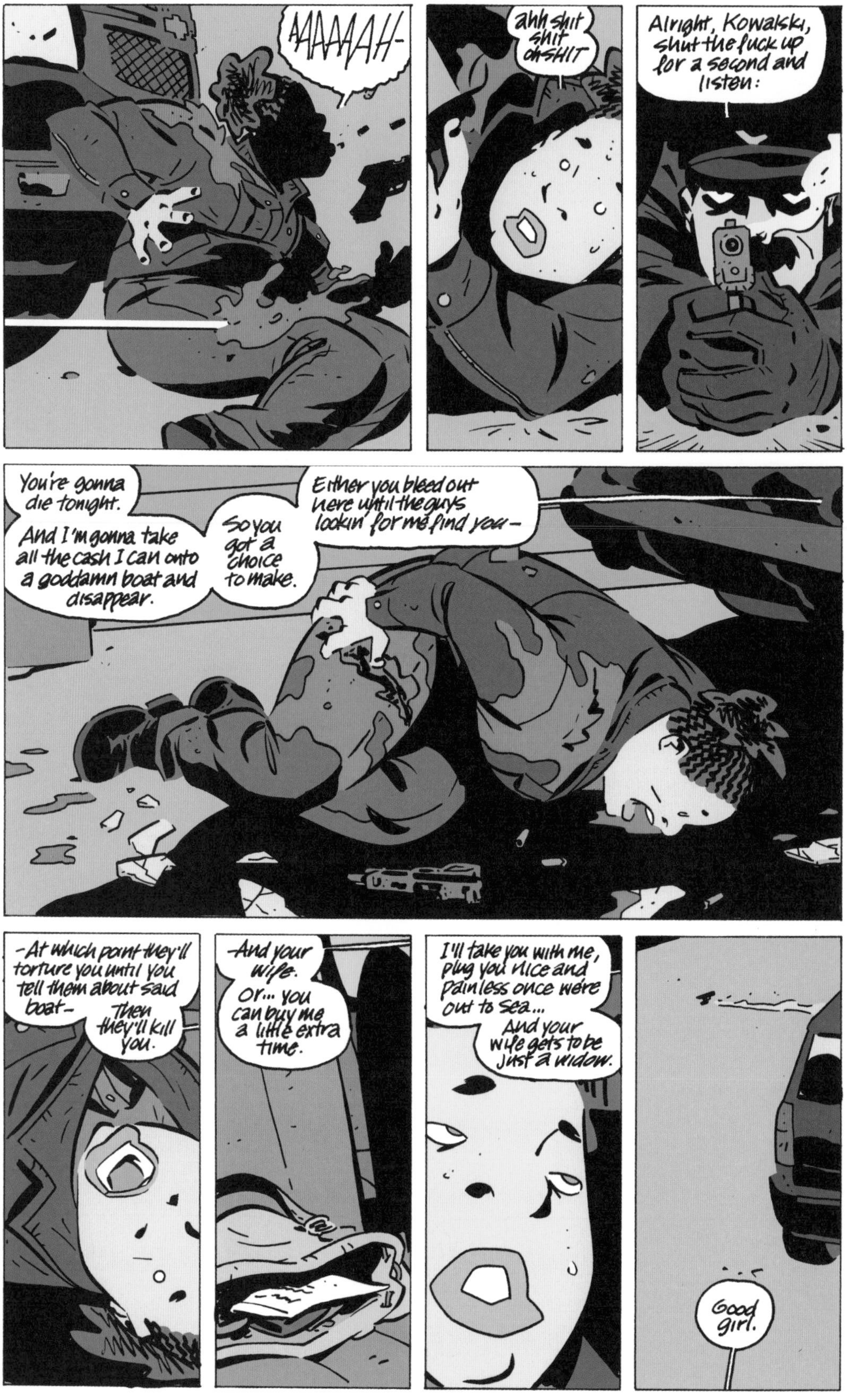
AAAAAAH-
ahh shit shit ohSHIT
Alright, Kowalski, shut the fuck up for a second and listen:
You're gonna die tonight.
And I'm gonna take all the cash I can onto a goddamn boat and disappear.
So you got a choice to make.
Either you bleed out here until the guys lookin' for me find you-
-At which point they'll torture you until you tell them about said boat-
Then they'll kill you.
-And your wife.
Or... you can buy me a little extra time.
I'll take you with me, plug you nice and painless once we're out to sea...
And your wife gets to be just a widow.
Good girl.

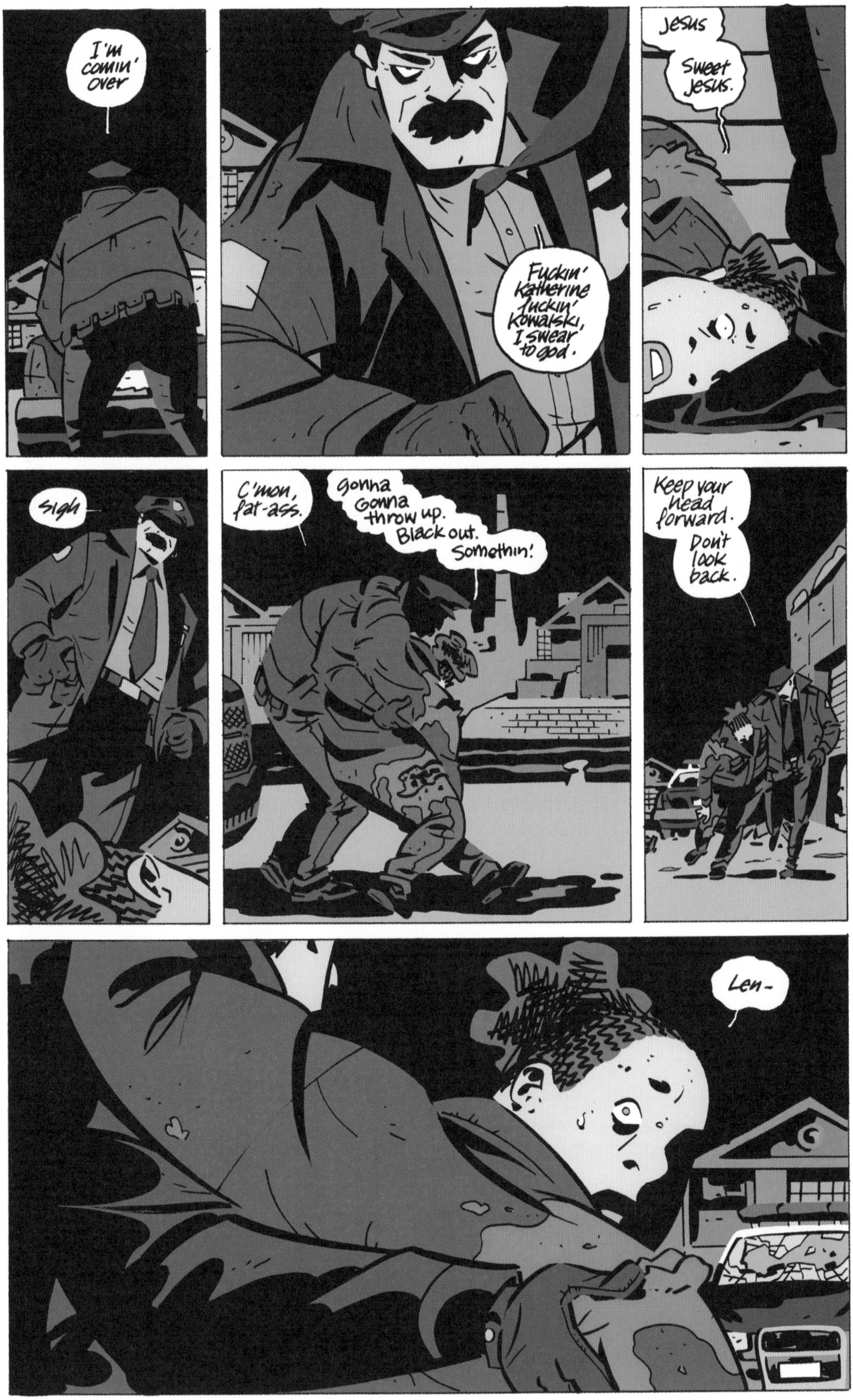

I'm comin' over
Fuckin' Katherine fuckin' Kowalski, I swear to god.
Jesus
Sweet Jesus.
sigh
C'mon, fat-ass.
Gonna Gonna throw up. Black out. Somethin'.
Keep your head forward.
Don't look back.
Len-

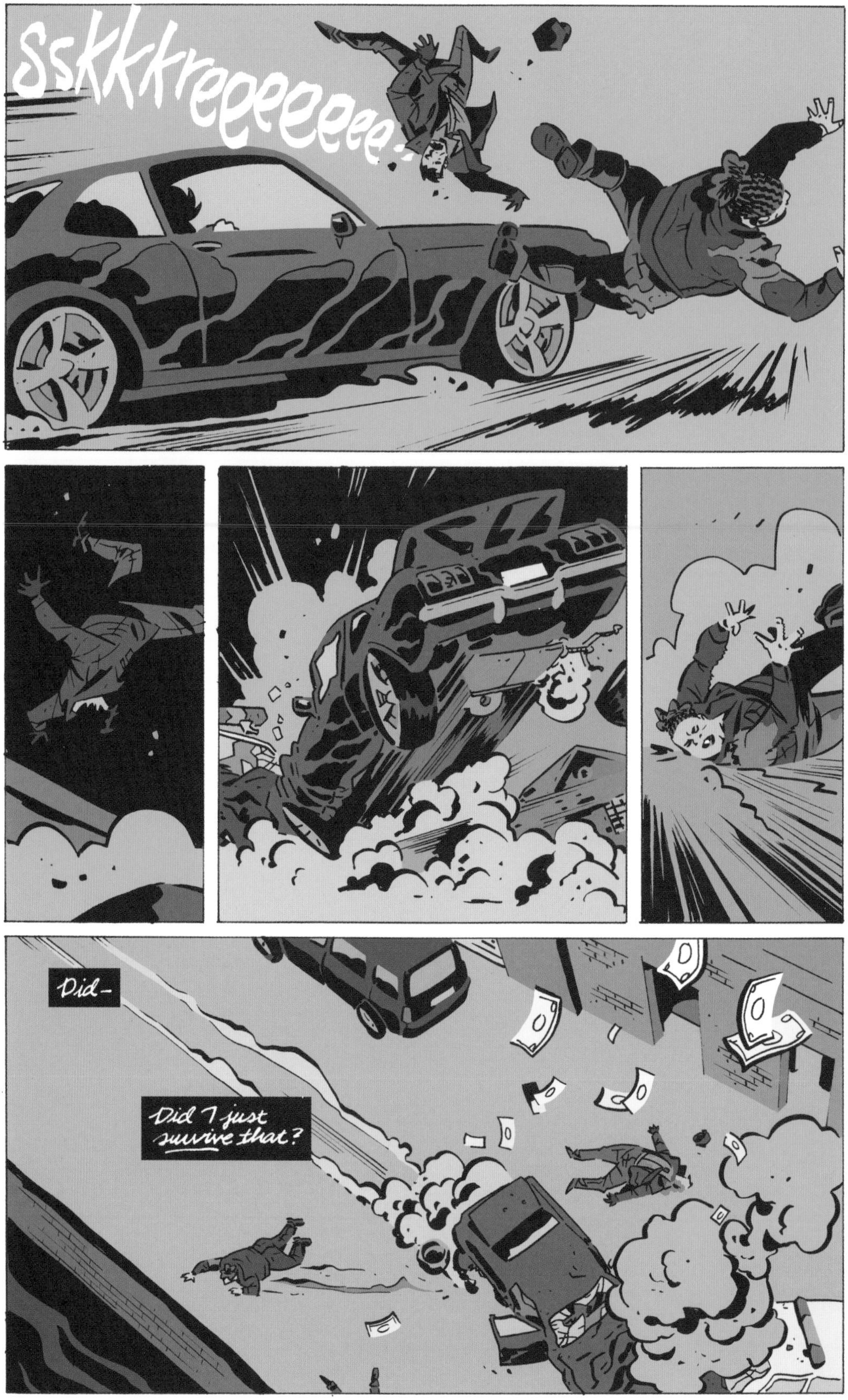
SSKKKREEEEEEEE--!
Did-
Did I just survive that?

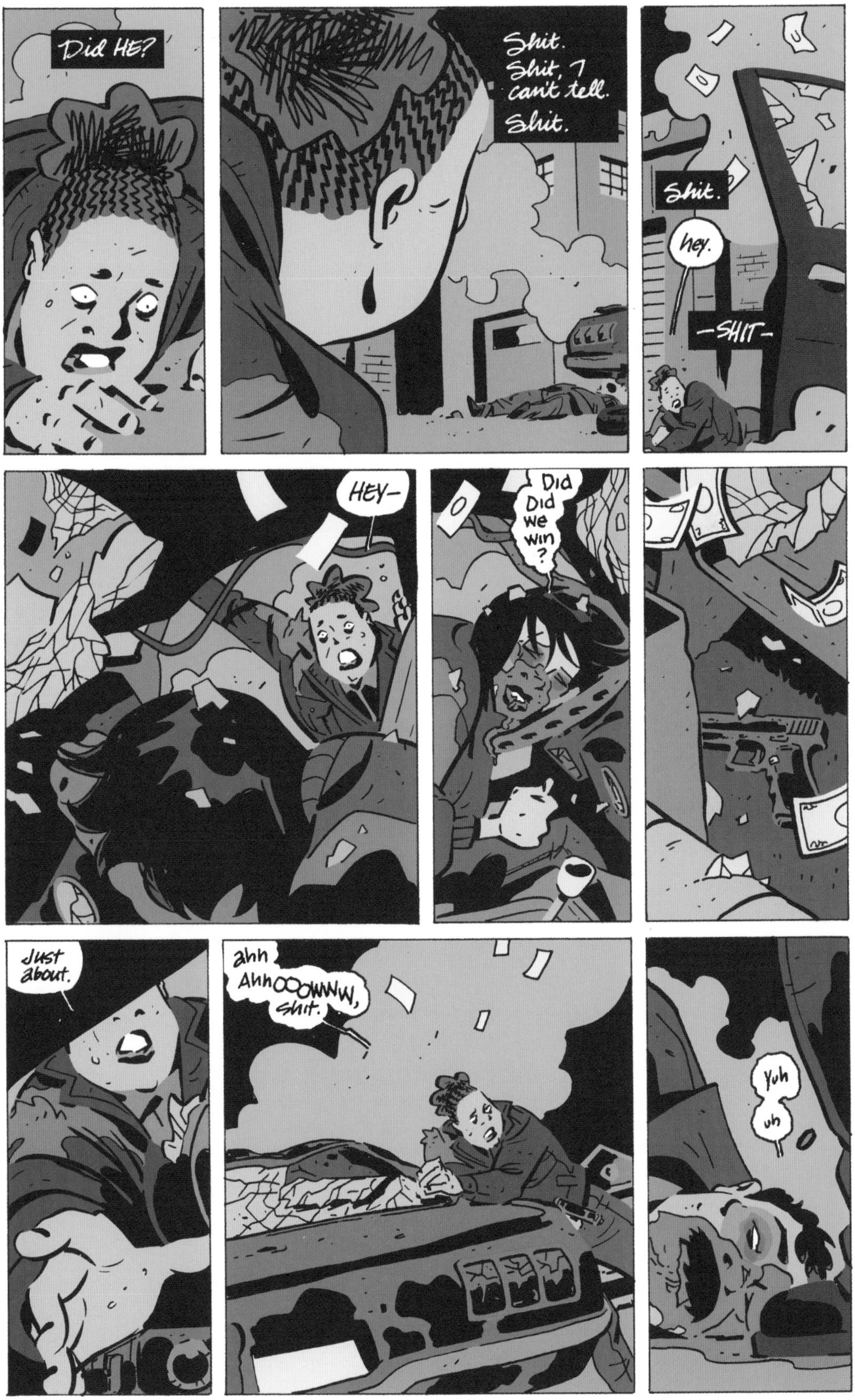
Did HE?
Shit.
Shit, I can't tell.
Shit.
Shit.
hey.
—SHIT—
HEY—
Did Did we win ?
Just about.
ahh Ahhooowww, shit.
yuh
uh

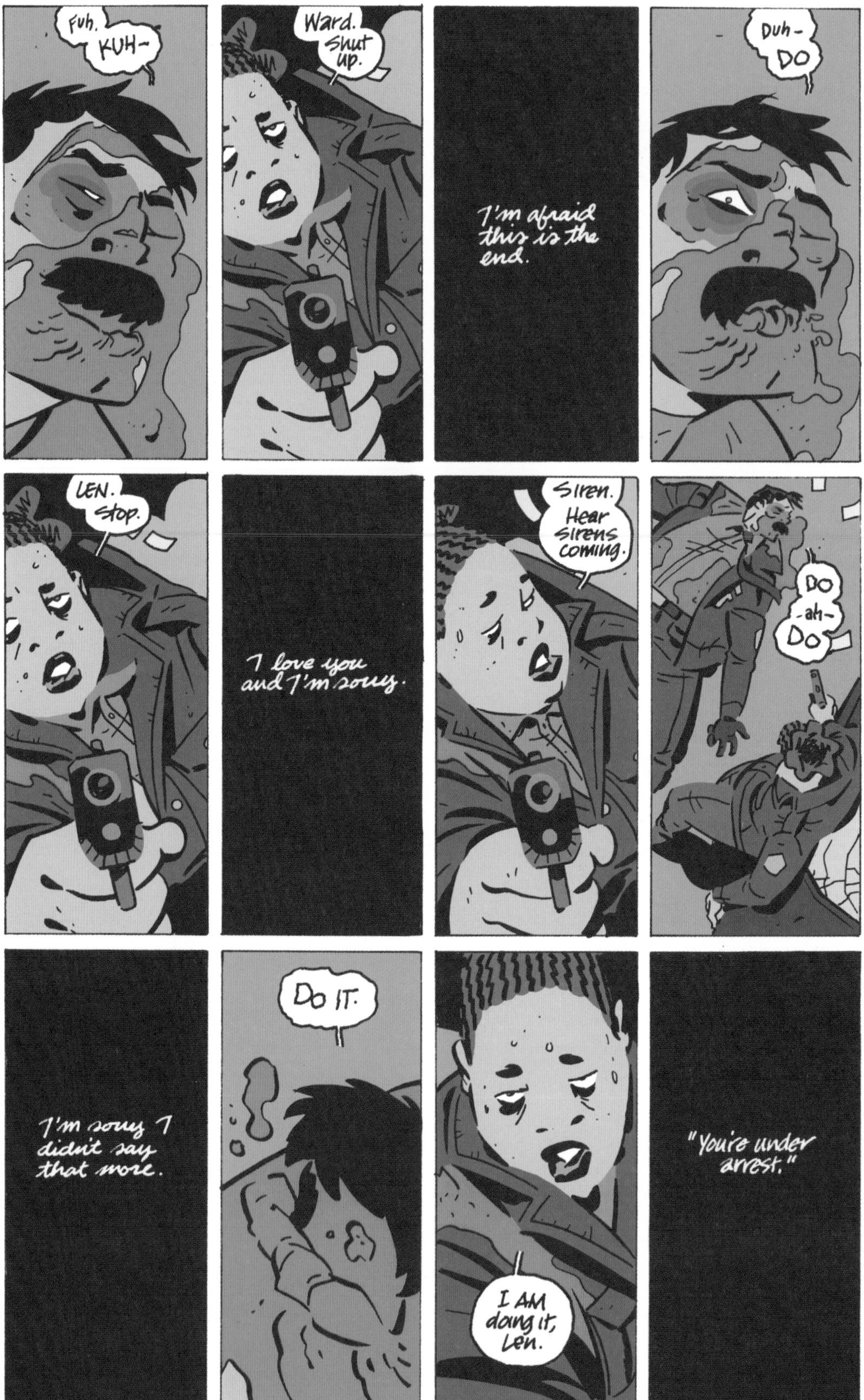

Fuh. KUH-
Ward. Shut up.
I'm afraid this is the end.
Duh- DO
LEN. Stop.
I love you and I'm sorry.
Siren. Hear sirens coming.
DO -ah- DO
I'm sorry I didn't say that more.
Do it.
I AM doing it, Len.
"You're under arrest."

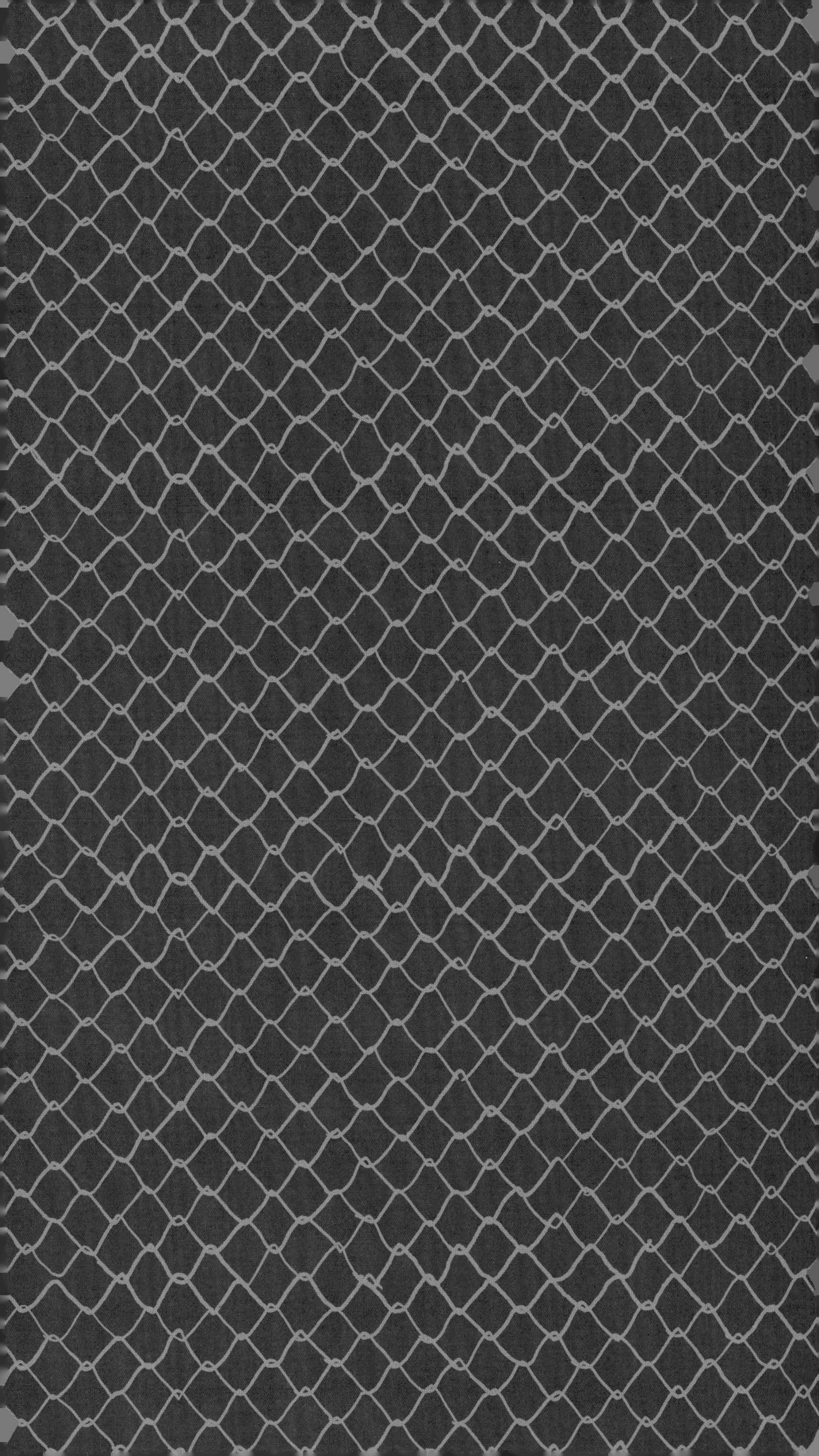

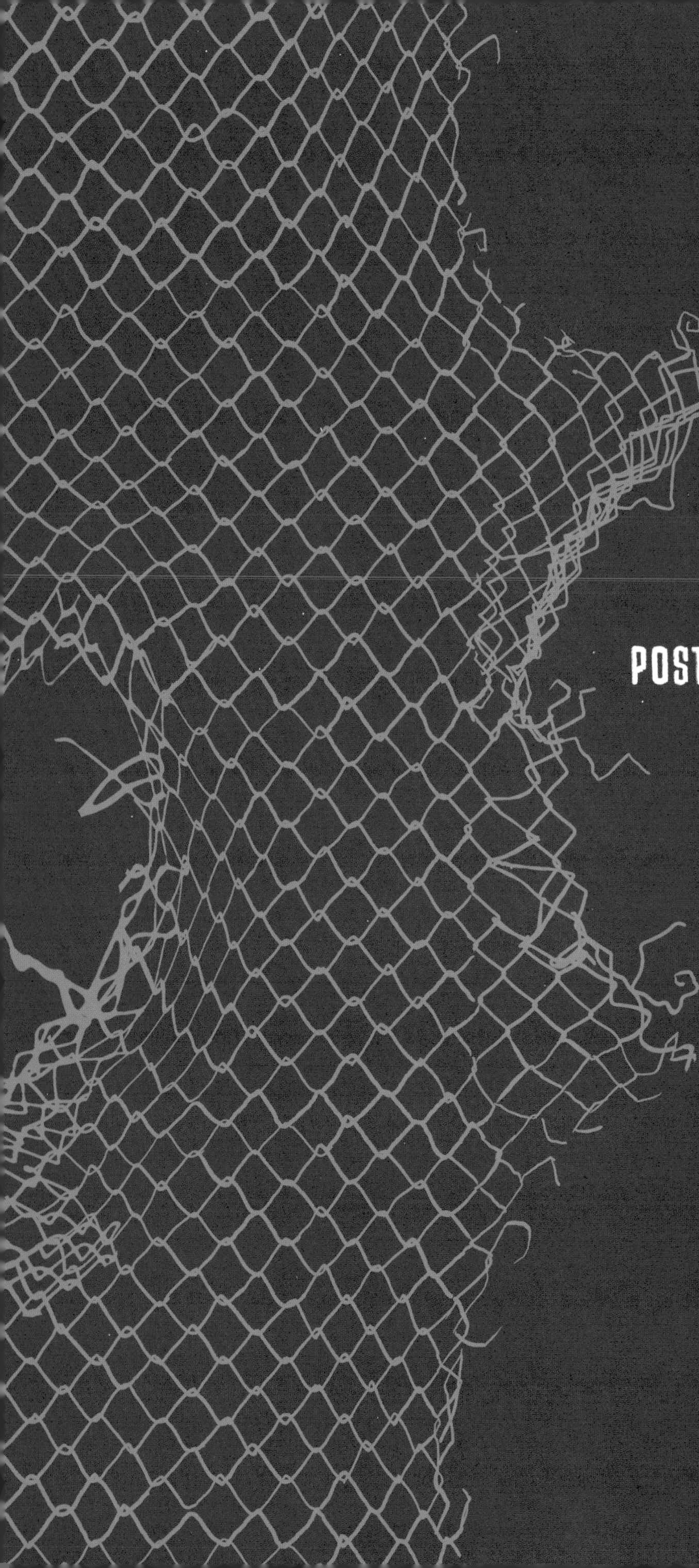

POSTSCRIPT I

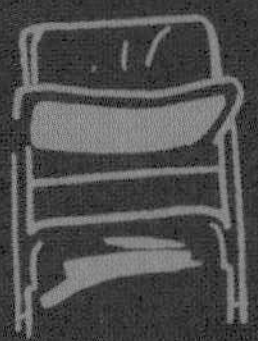

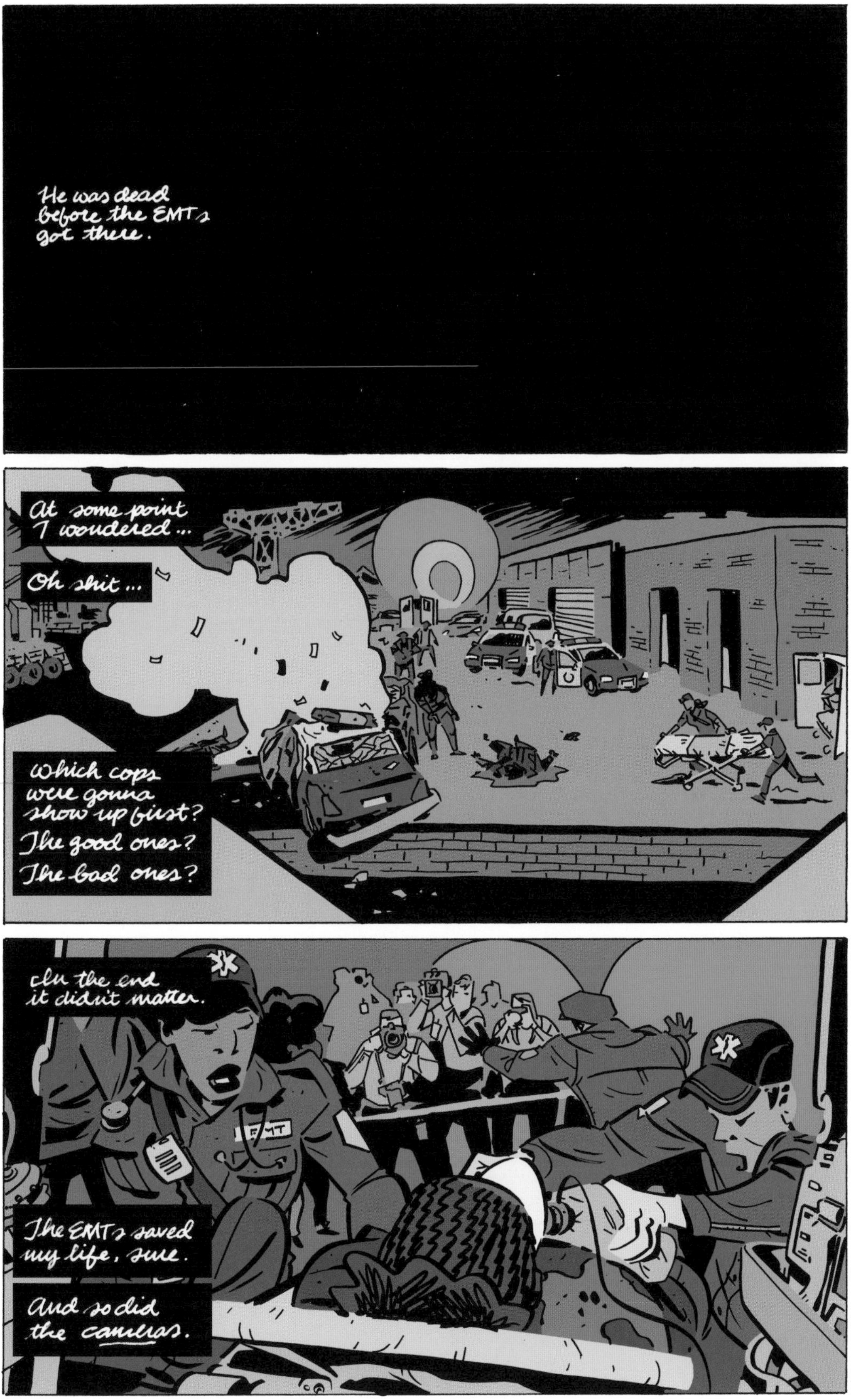
He was dead before the EMTs got there.
At some point I wondered...
Oh shit...
Which cops were gonna show up first?
The good ones?
The bad ones?
In the end it didn't matter.
EMT
The EMTs saved my life, sure.
And so did the cameras.

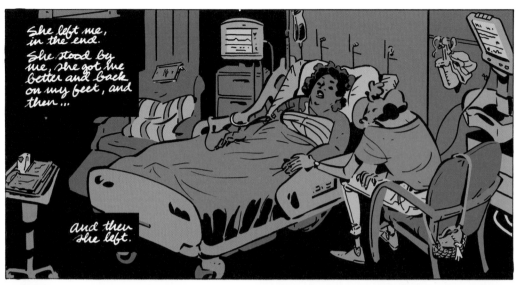

She left me, in the end.

She stood by me, she got me better and back on my feet, and then...

and then she left.

I didn't blame her.

Whatever person I'd become in that hospital, whoever I'd be when I left...

... I'd always be the woman that lied to her and broke her heart, time and time again.

No matter how many medals they pinned on me.

I wasn't a cop. I wasn't a wife. I wasn't a drunk anymore.

There wasn't anything left.

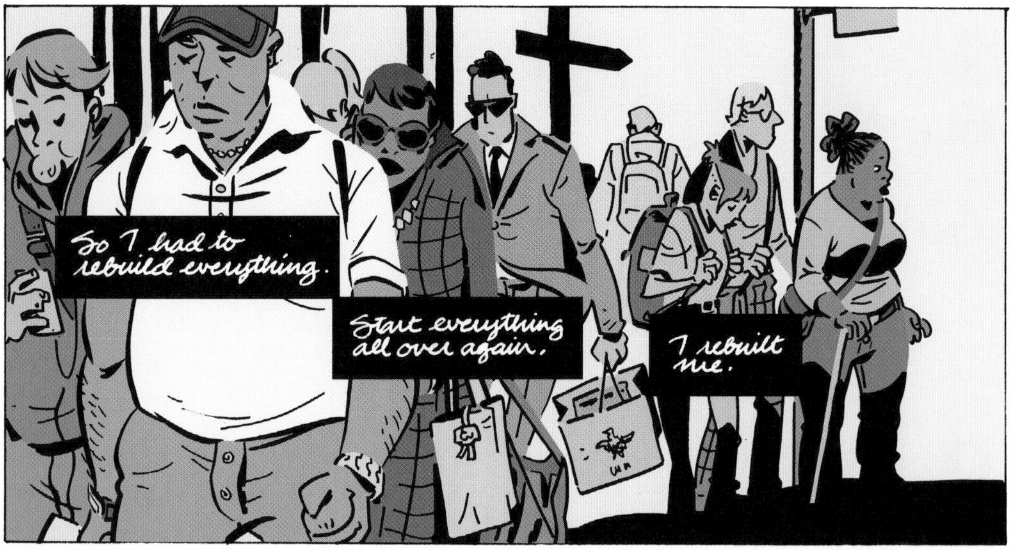
So I had to rebuild everything.
Start everything all over again.
I rebuilt me.

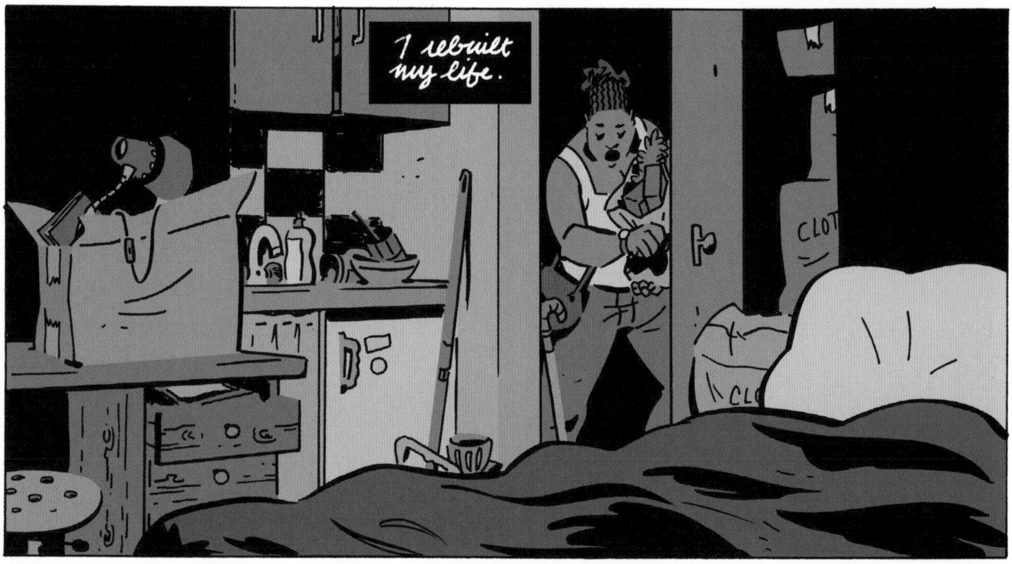
I rebuilt my life.

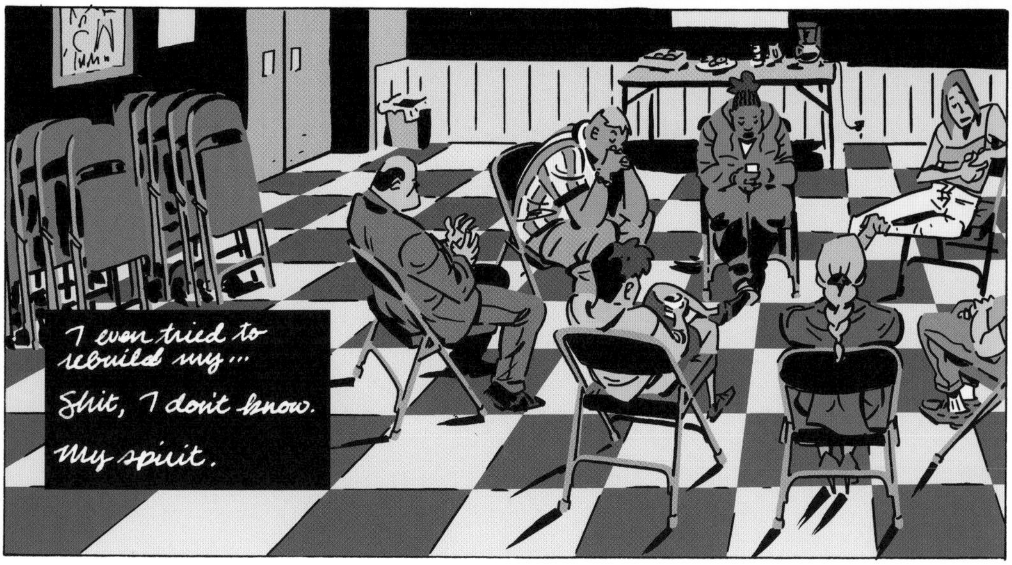
I even tried to rebuild my...
Shit, I don't know.
My spirit.

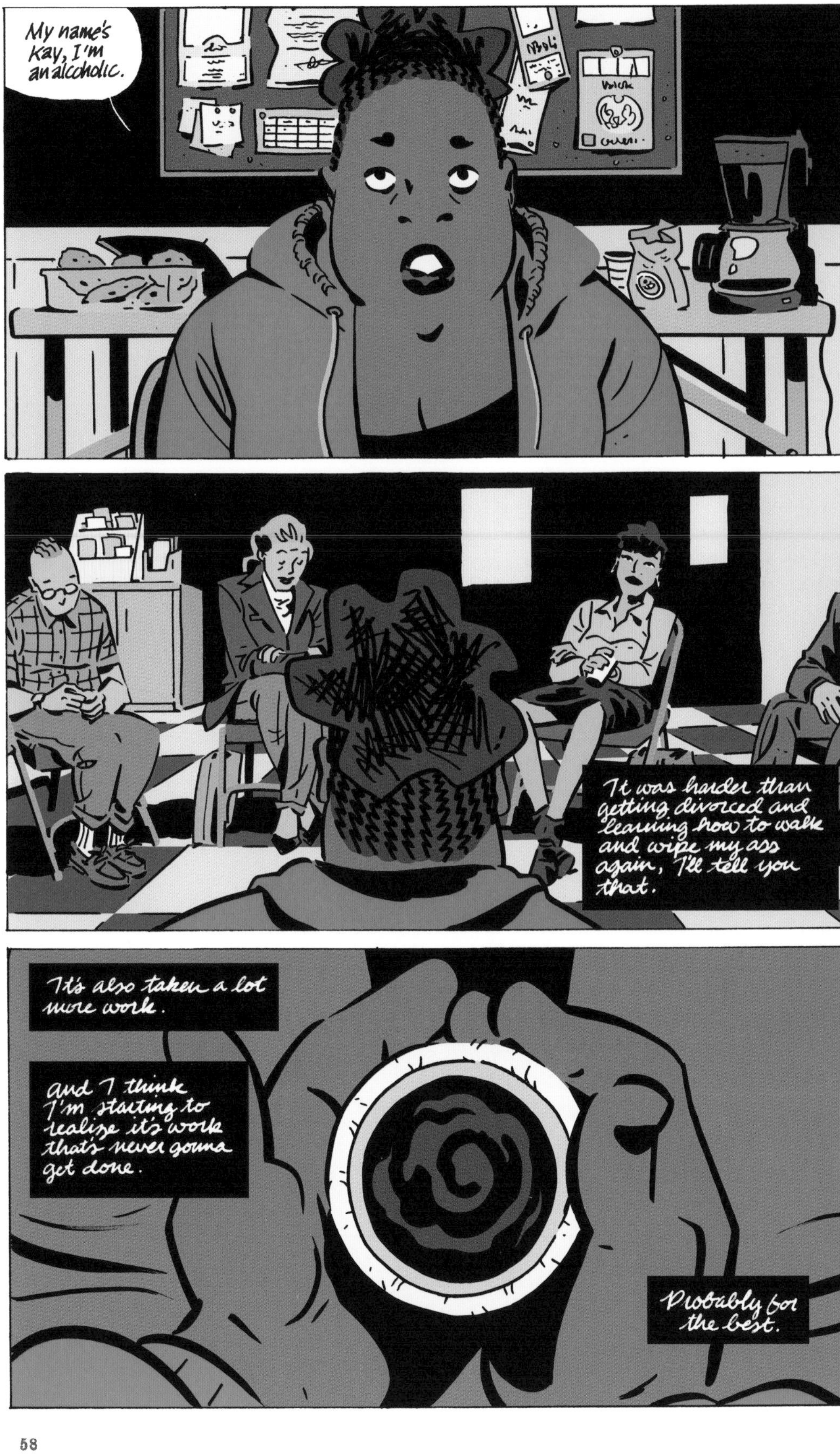
My name's Kay, I'm an alcoholic.
It was harder than getting divorced and learning how to walk and wipe my ass again, I'll tell you that.
It's also taken a lot more work.
And I think I'm starting to realize it's work that's never gonna get done.
Probably for the best.

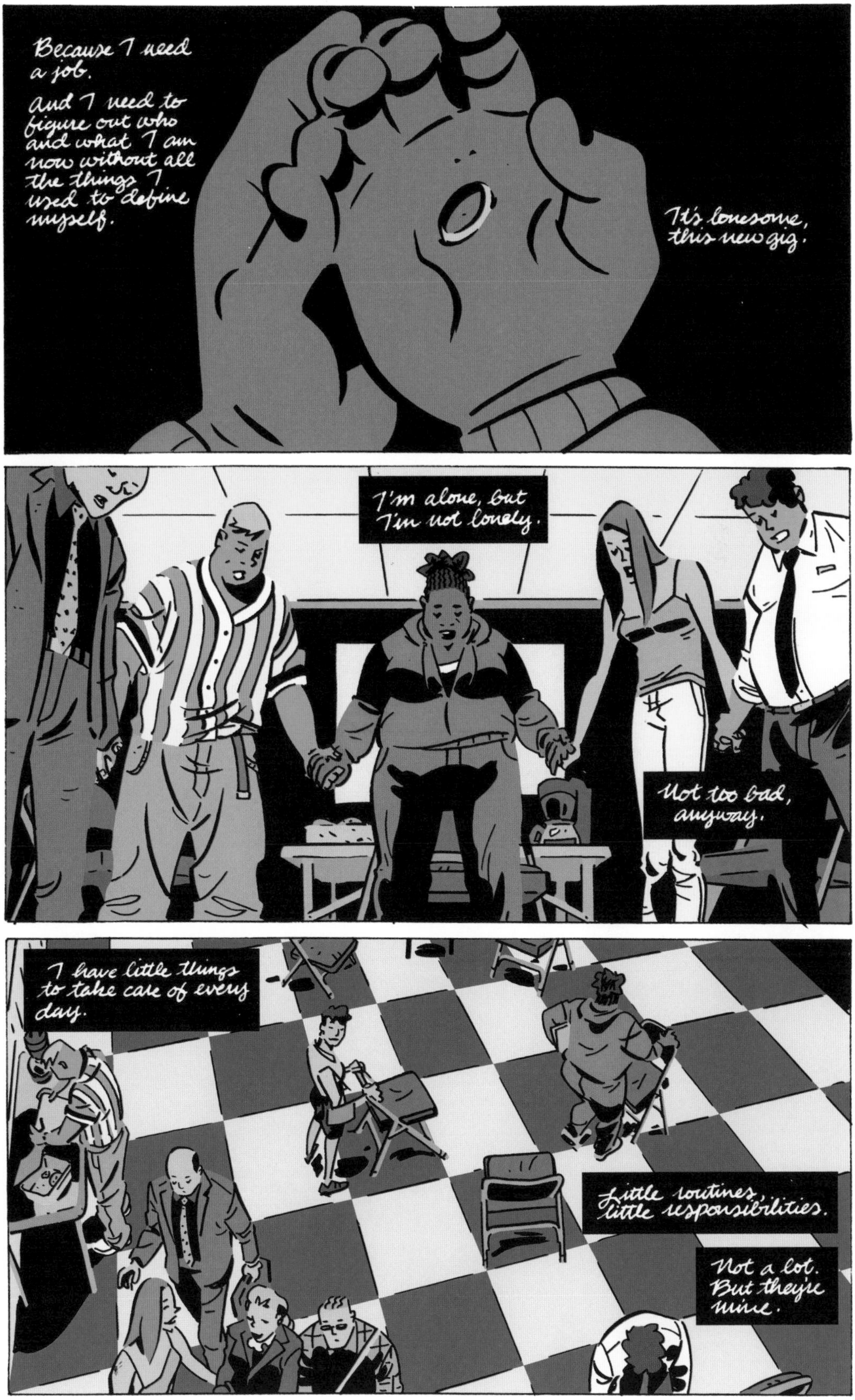
Because I need a job.
And I need to figure out who and what I am now without all the things I used to define myself.
It's lonesome, this new gig.
I'm alone, but I'm not lonely.
Not too bad, anyway.
I have little things to take care of every day.
Little routines, little responsibilities.
Not a lot. But they're mine.

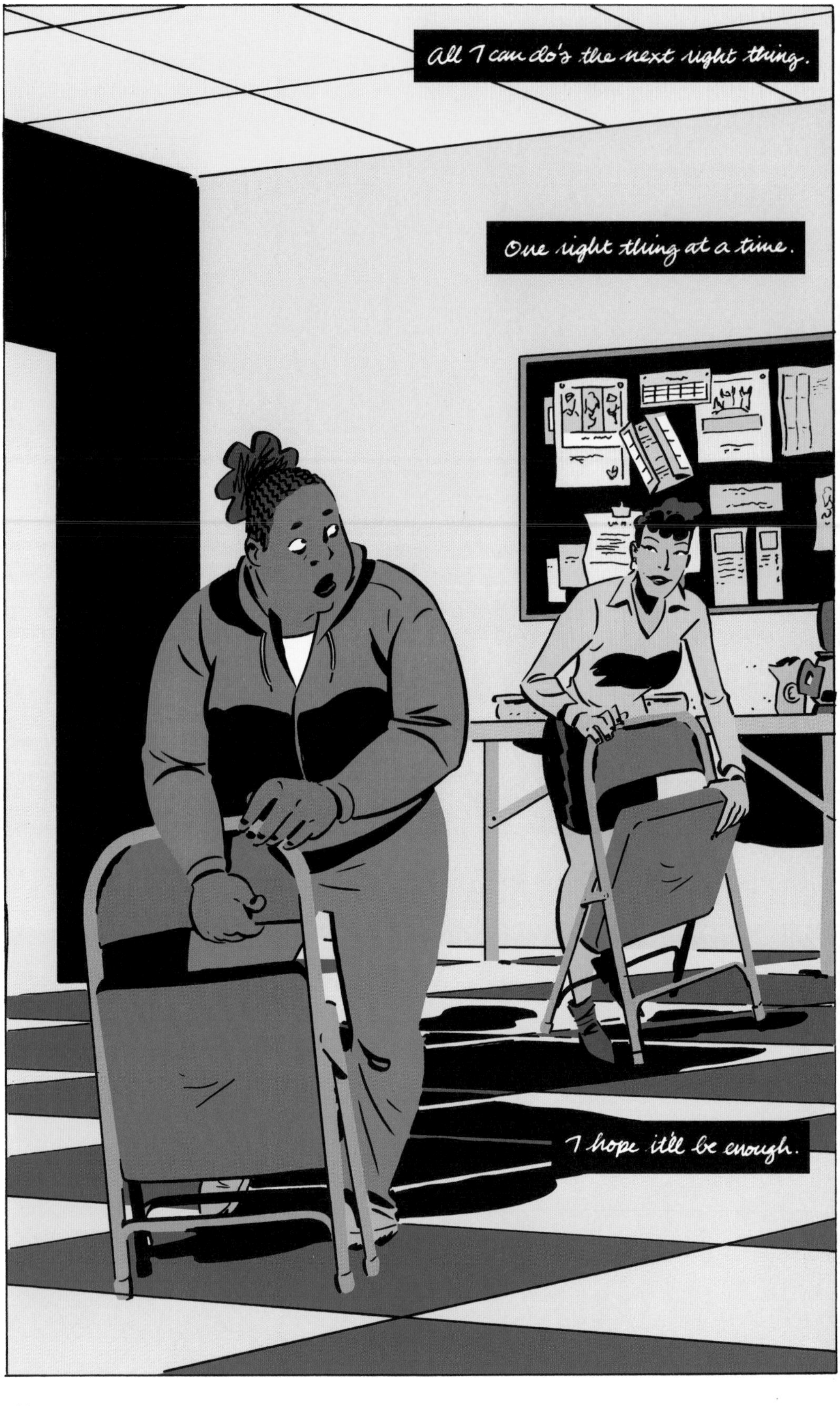
All I can do's the next right thing.
One right thing at a time.
I hope it'll be enough.

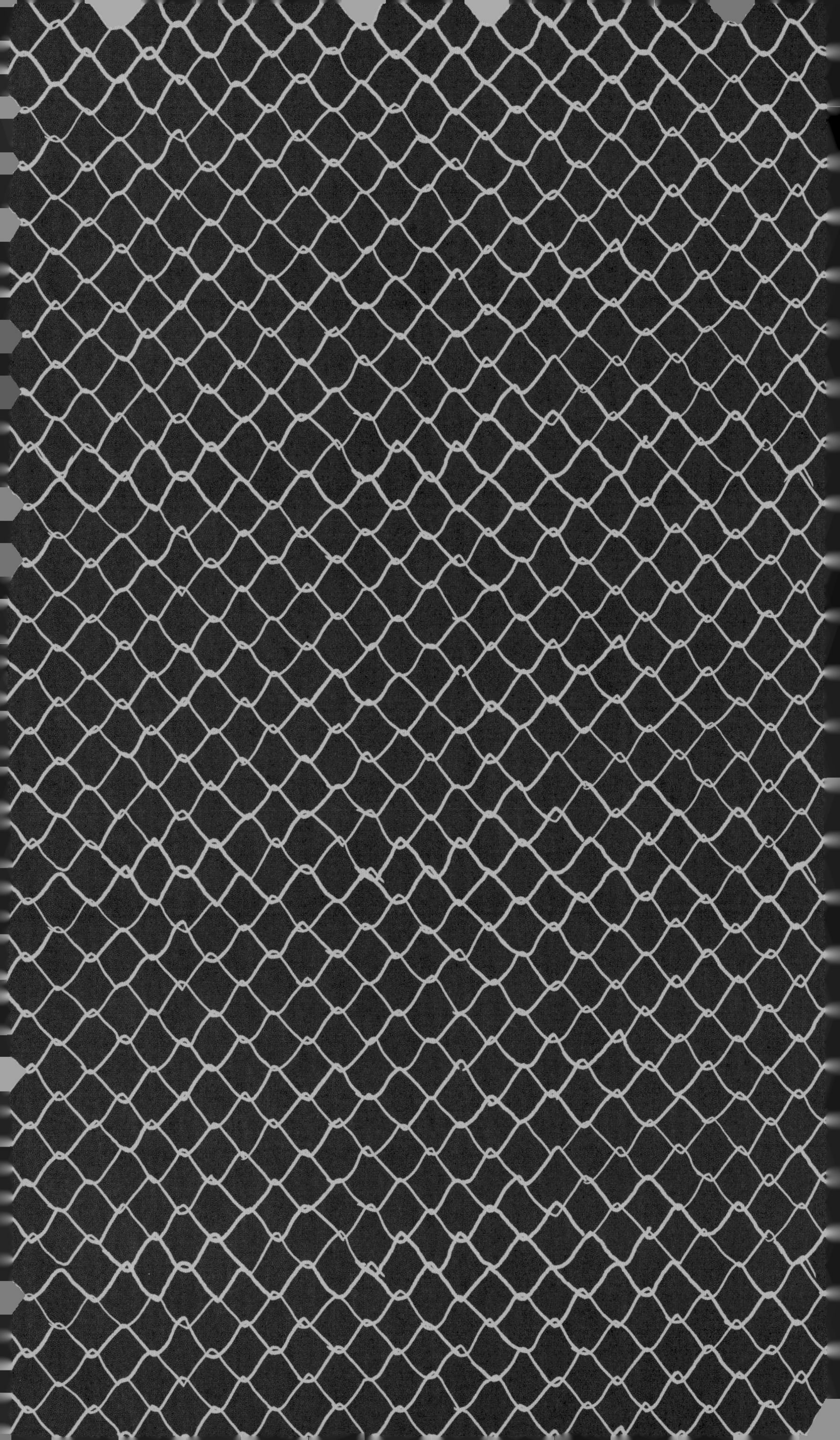

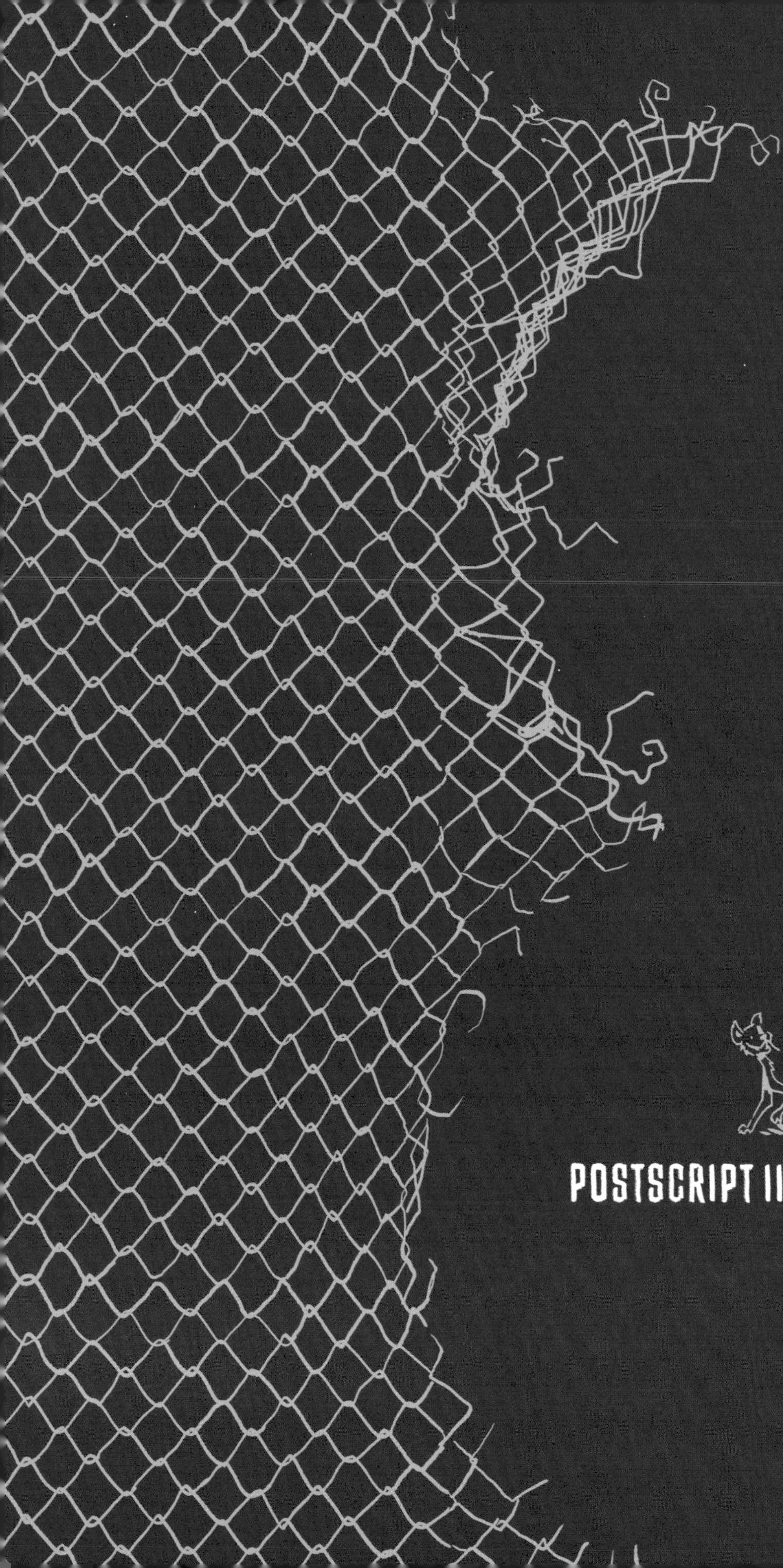

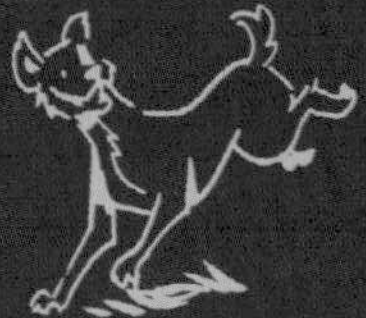

POSTSCRIPT II

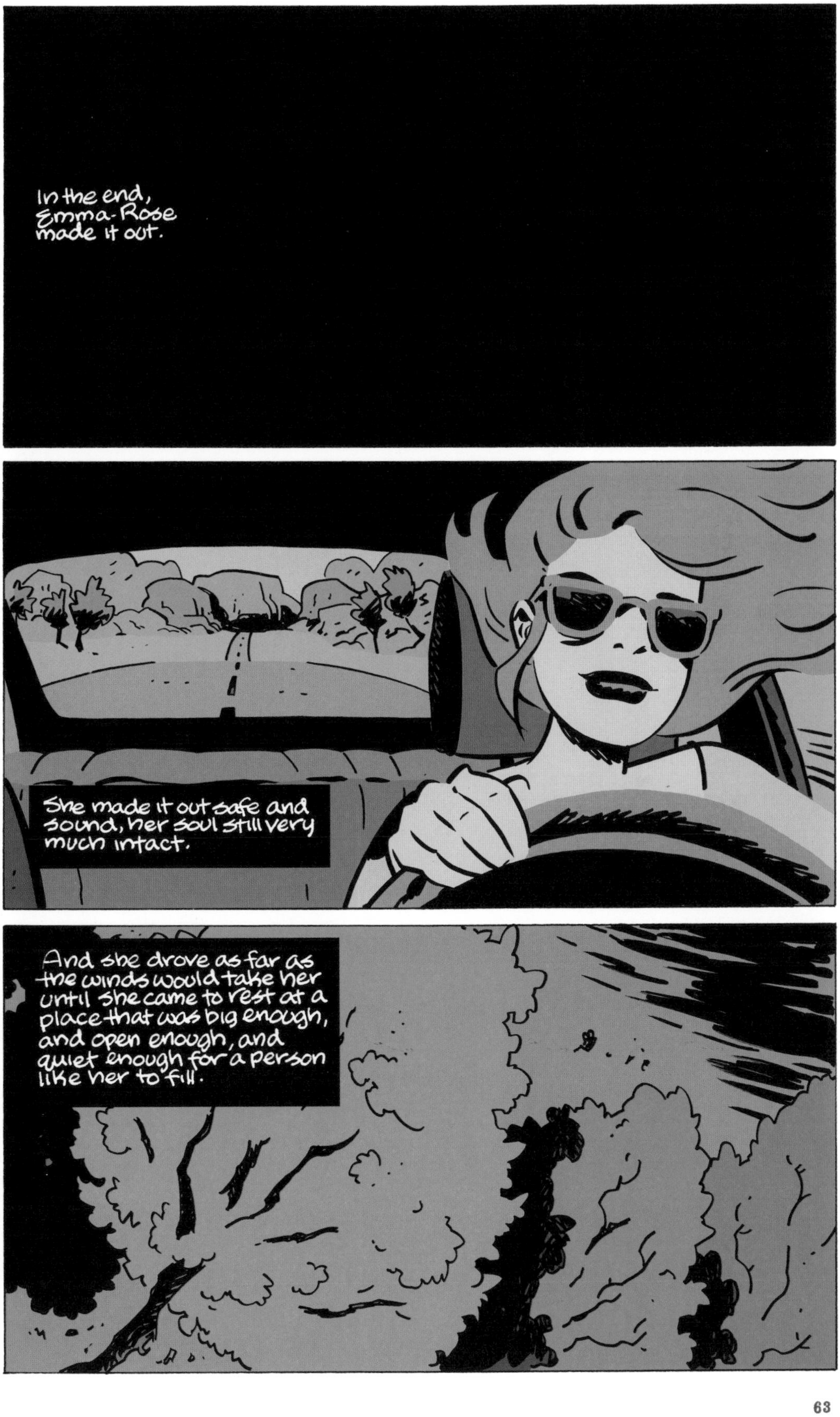
In the end, Emma-Rose made it out.
She made it out safe and sound, her soul still very much intact.
And she drove as far as the winds would take her until she came to rest at a place that was big enough, and open enough, and quiet enough for a person like her to fill.

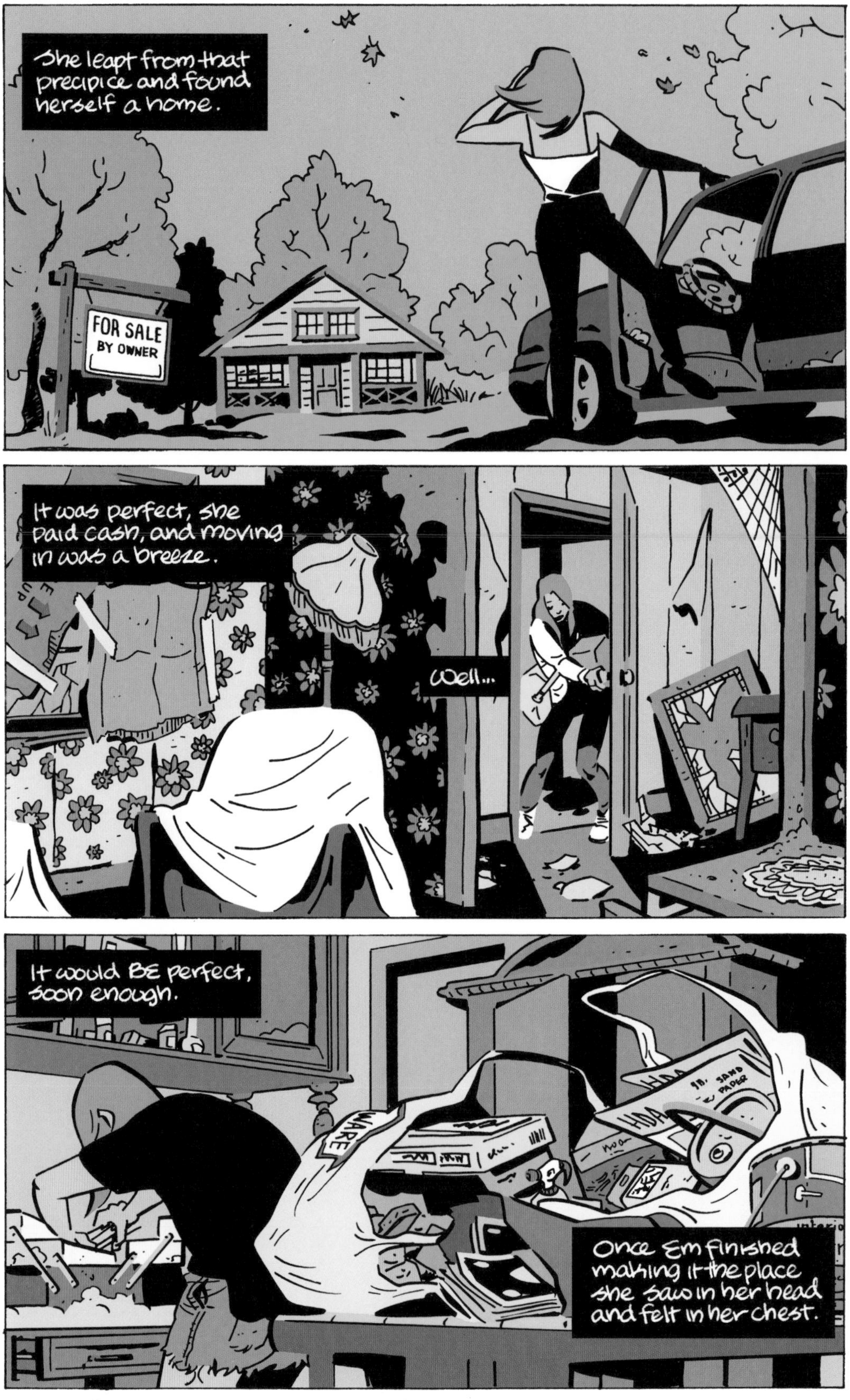
She leapt from that precipice and found herself a home.
FOR SALE
BY OWNER
It was perfect, she paid cash, and moving in was a breeze.
Well...
It would BE perfect, soon enough.
WARE
Once Em finished making it the place she saw in her head and felt in her chest.

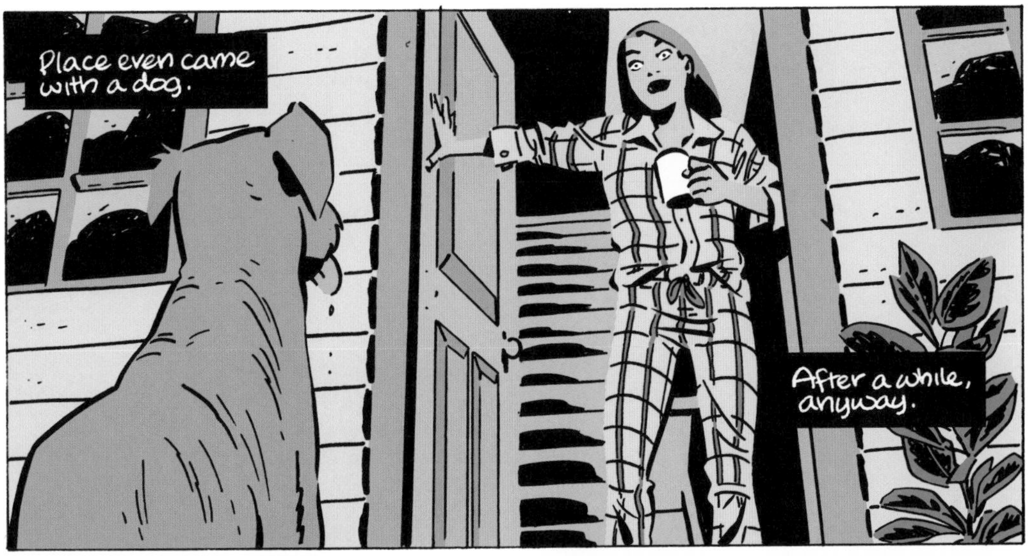
Place even came with a dog.
After a while, anyway.

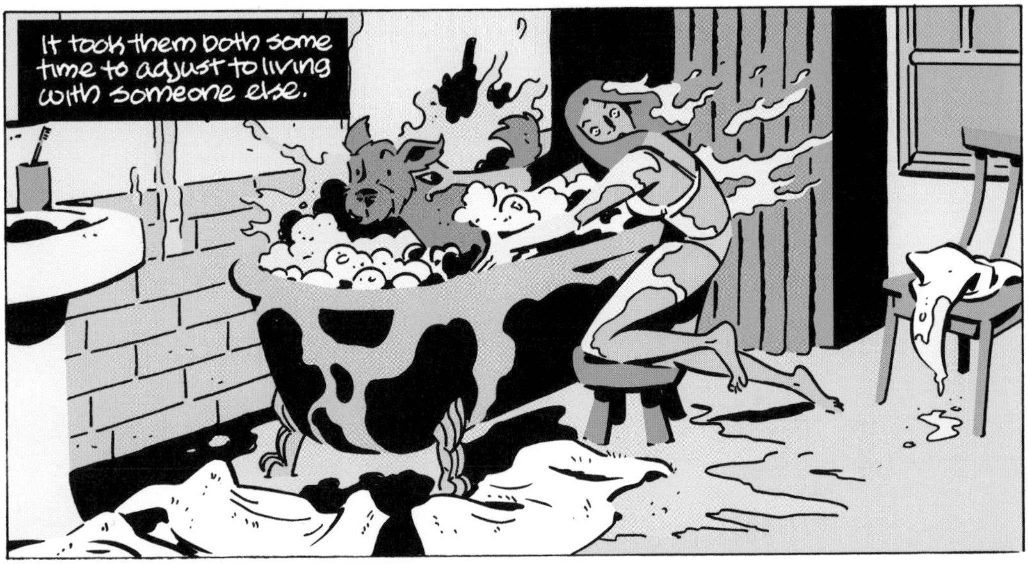
It took them both some time to adjust to living with someone else.

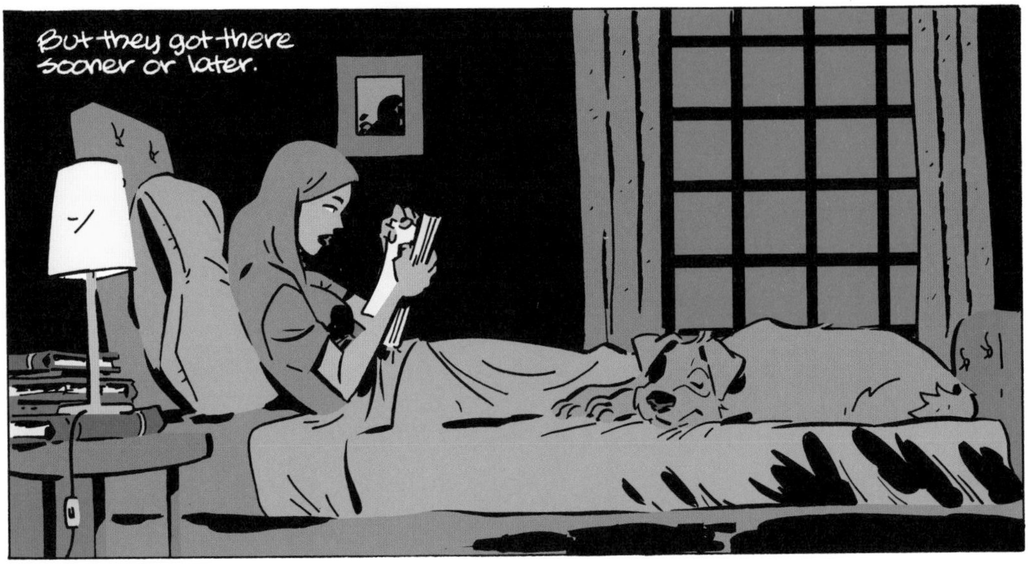
But they got there sooner or later.

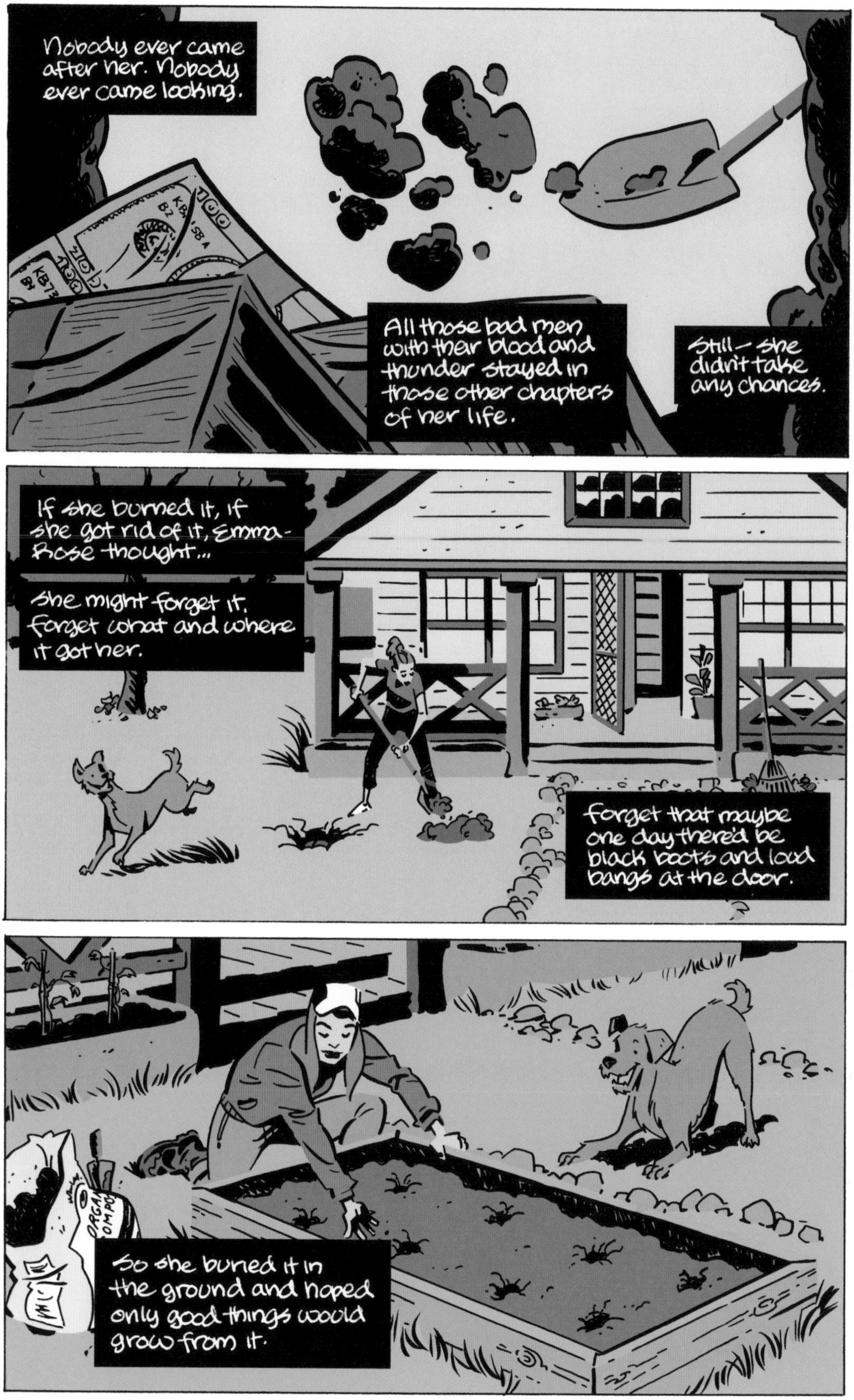
Nobody ever came after her. Nobody ever came looking.
All those bad men with their blood and thunder stayed in those other chapters of her life.
Still— she didn't take any chances.
If she burned it, if she got rid of it, Emma-Rose thought...
she might forget it. Forget what and where it got her.
Forget that maybe one day there'd be black boots and loud bangs at the door.
So she buried it in the ground and hoped only good things would grow from it.

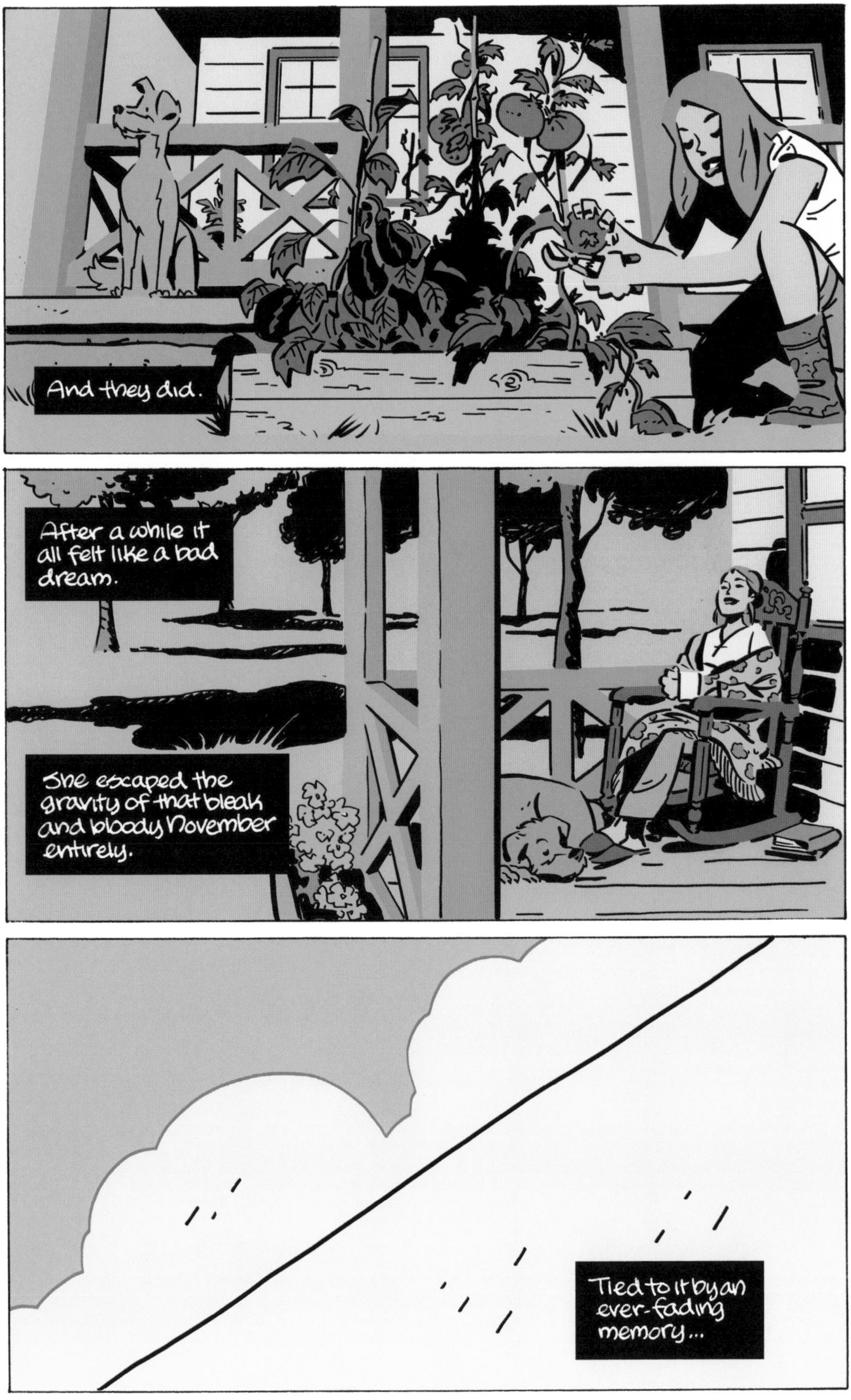
And they did.
After a while it all felt like a bad dream.
She escaped the gravity of that bleak and bloody November entirely.
Tied to it by an ever-fading memory...

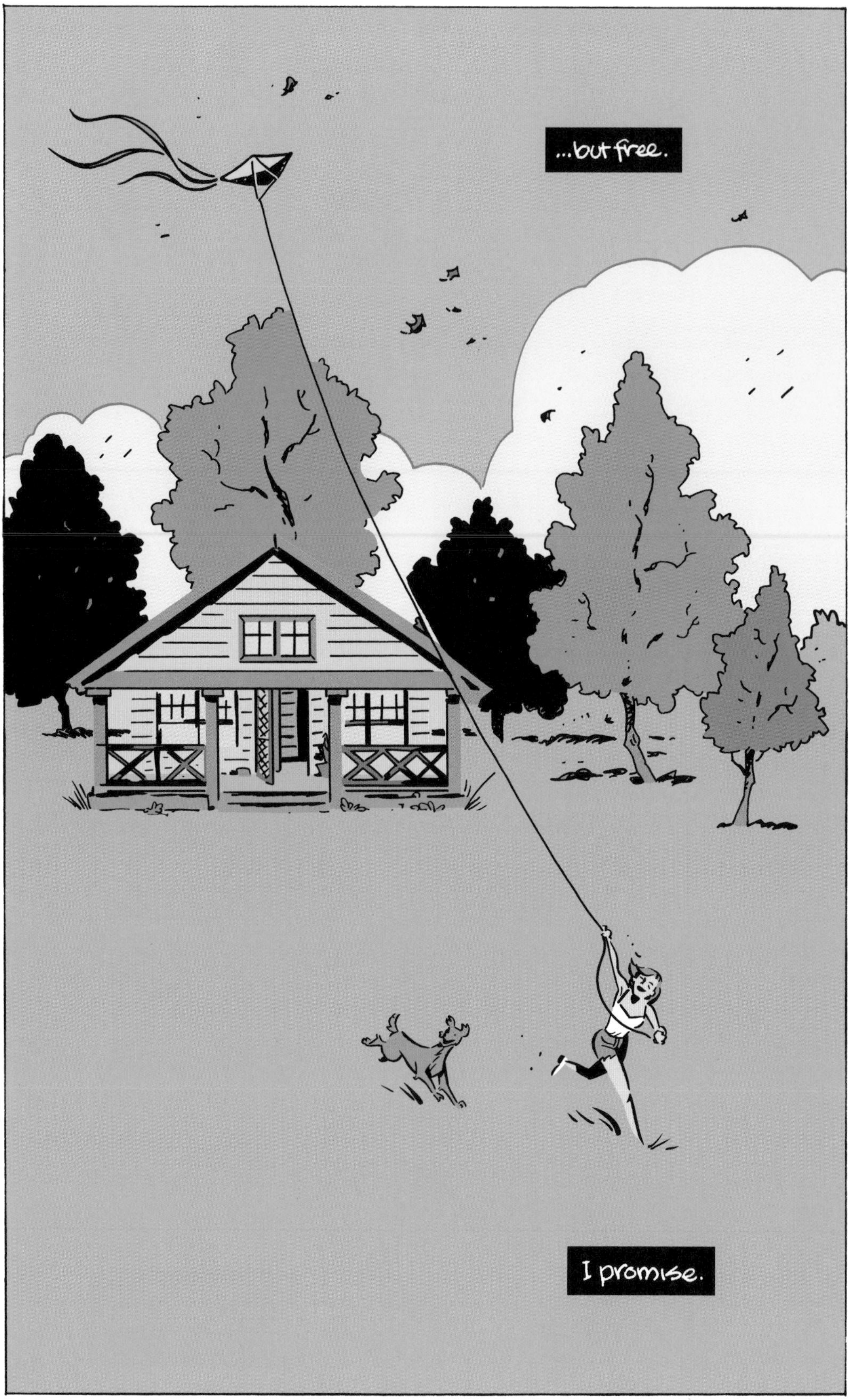
...but free.
I promise.

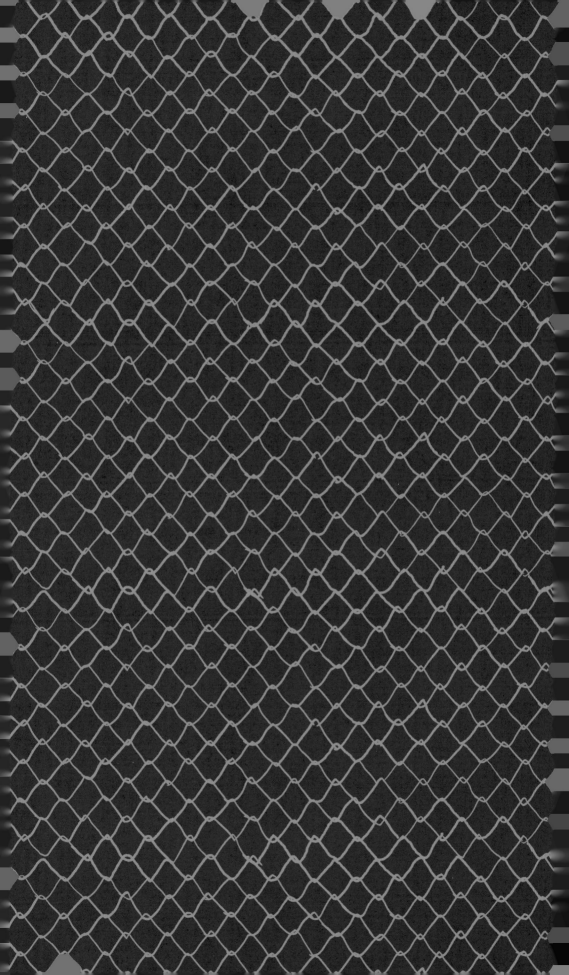

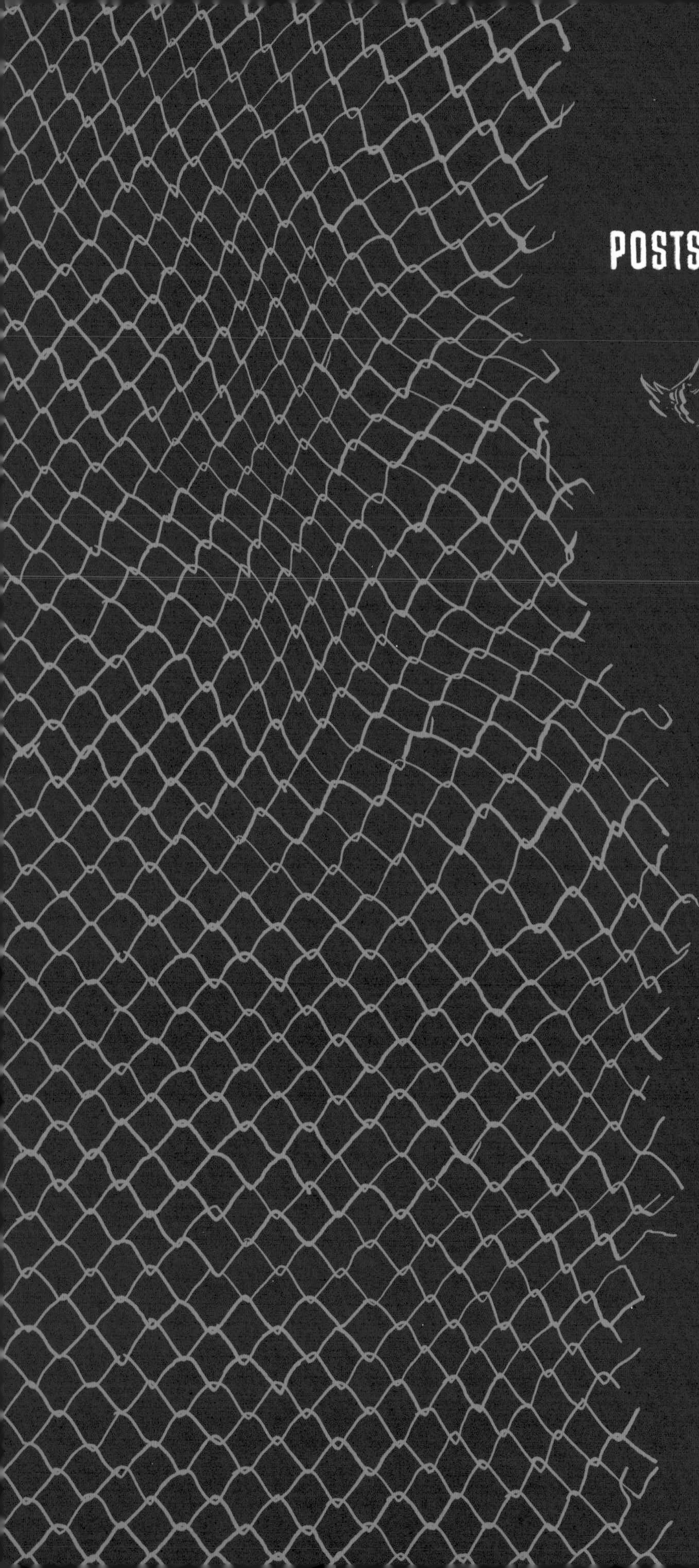

POSTSCRIPT III

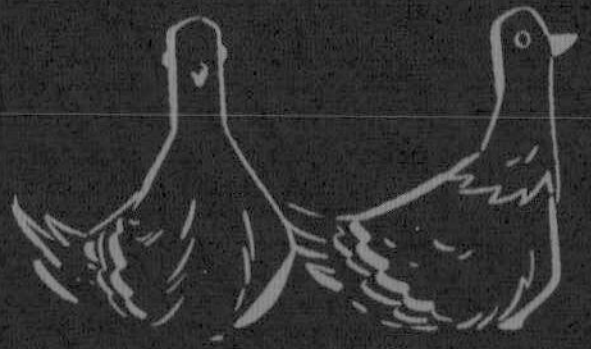

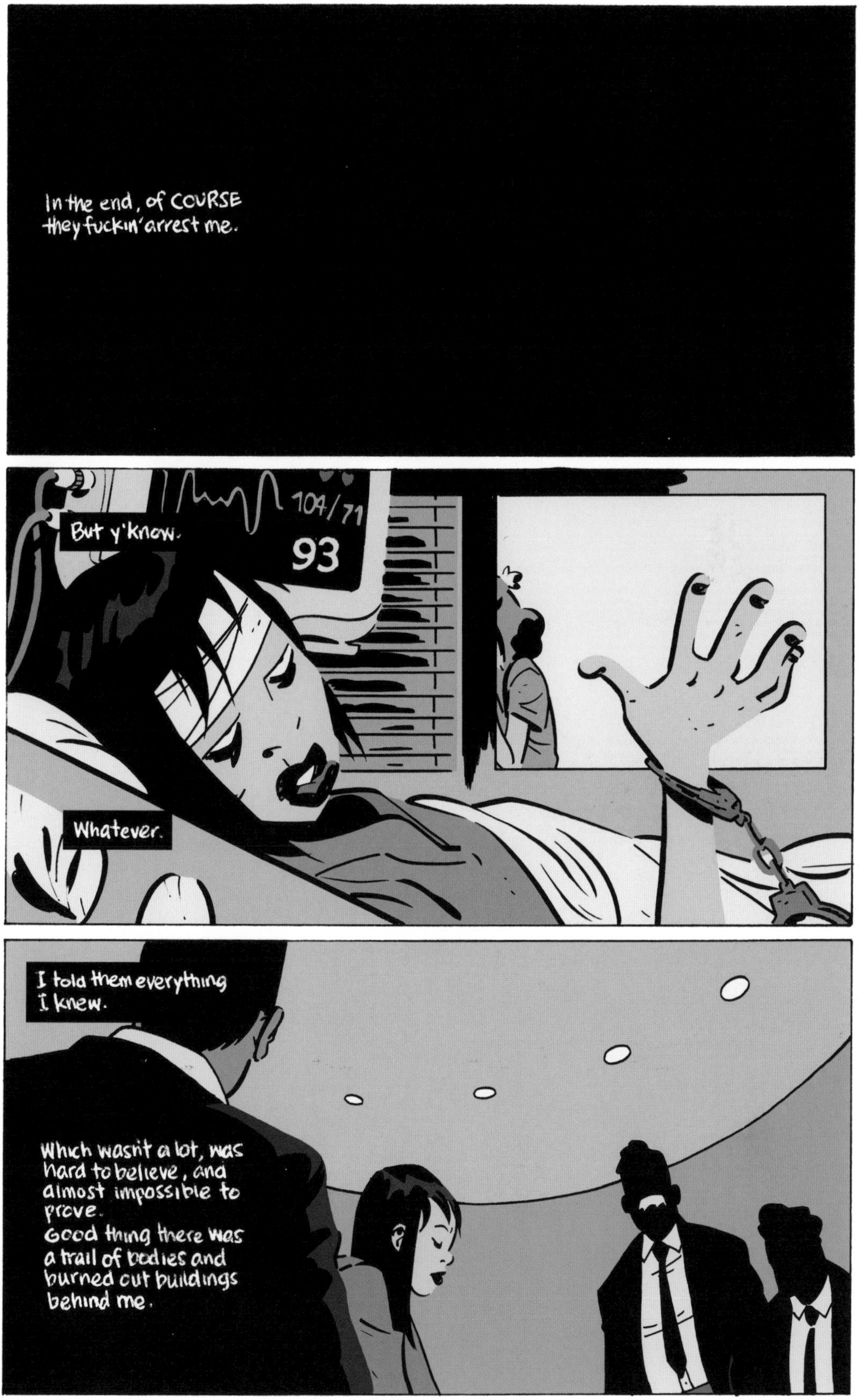
In the end, of COURSE they fuckin' arrest me.
104/71
93
But y'know.
Whatever.
I told them everything I knew.
Which wasn't a lot, was hard to believe, and almost impossible to prove.
Good thing there was a trail of bodies and burned out buildings behind me.

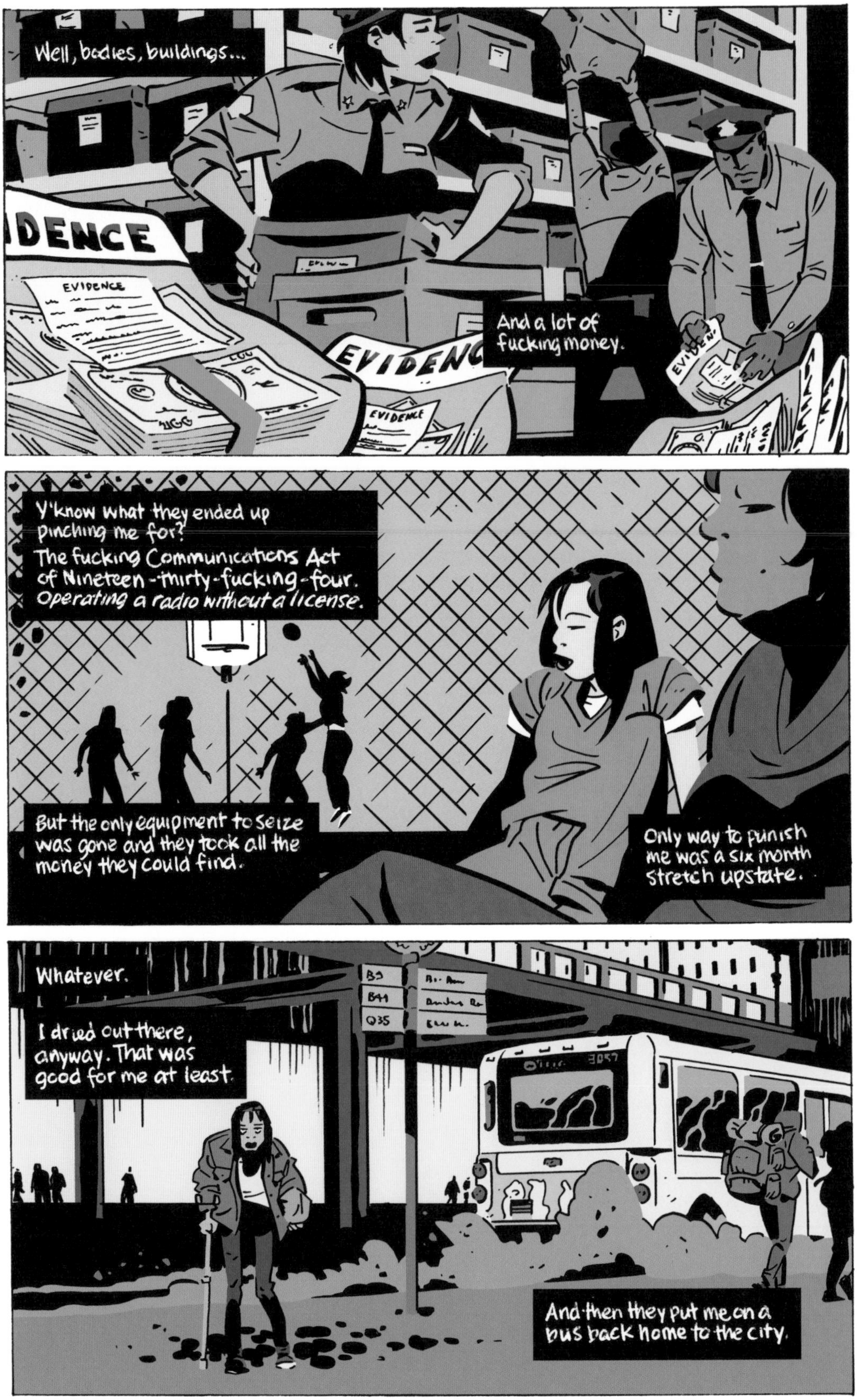

Well, bodies, buildings...
EVIDENCE
And a lot of fucking money.
Y'know what they ended up pinching me for?
The fucking Communications Act of Nineteen-thirty-fucking-four. Operating a radio without a license.
But the only equipment to seize was gone and they took all the money they could find.
Only way to punish me was a six month stretch upstate.
Whatever.
I dried out there, anyway. That was good for me at least.
B9
B41
Q35
3057
And then they put me on a bus back home to the city.

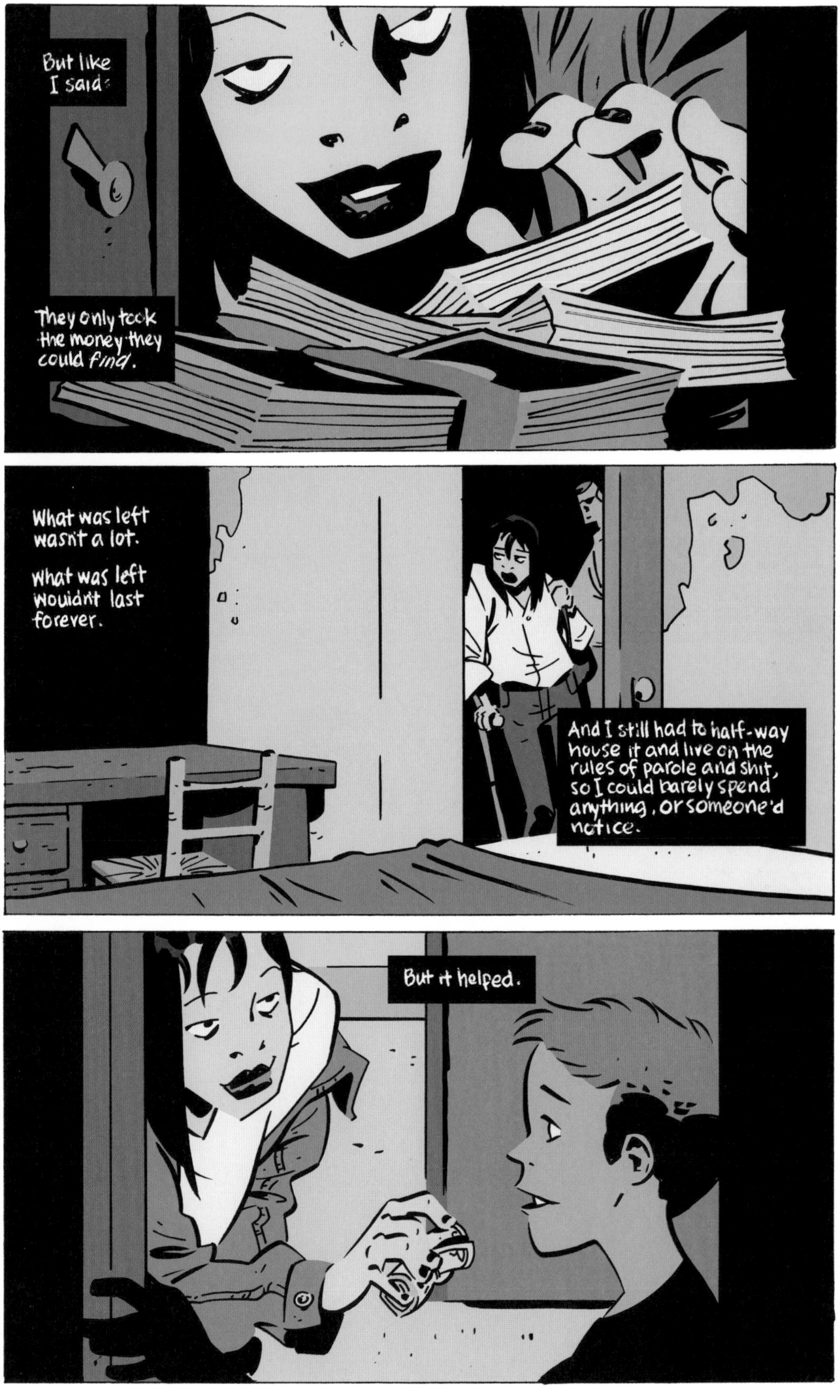
But like I said:
They only took the money they could *find*.
What was left wasn't a lot.
What was left wouldn't last forever.
And I still had to half-way house it and live on the rules of parole and shit, so I could barely spend anything, or someone'd notice.
But it helped.

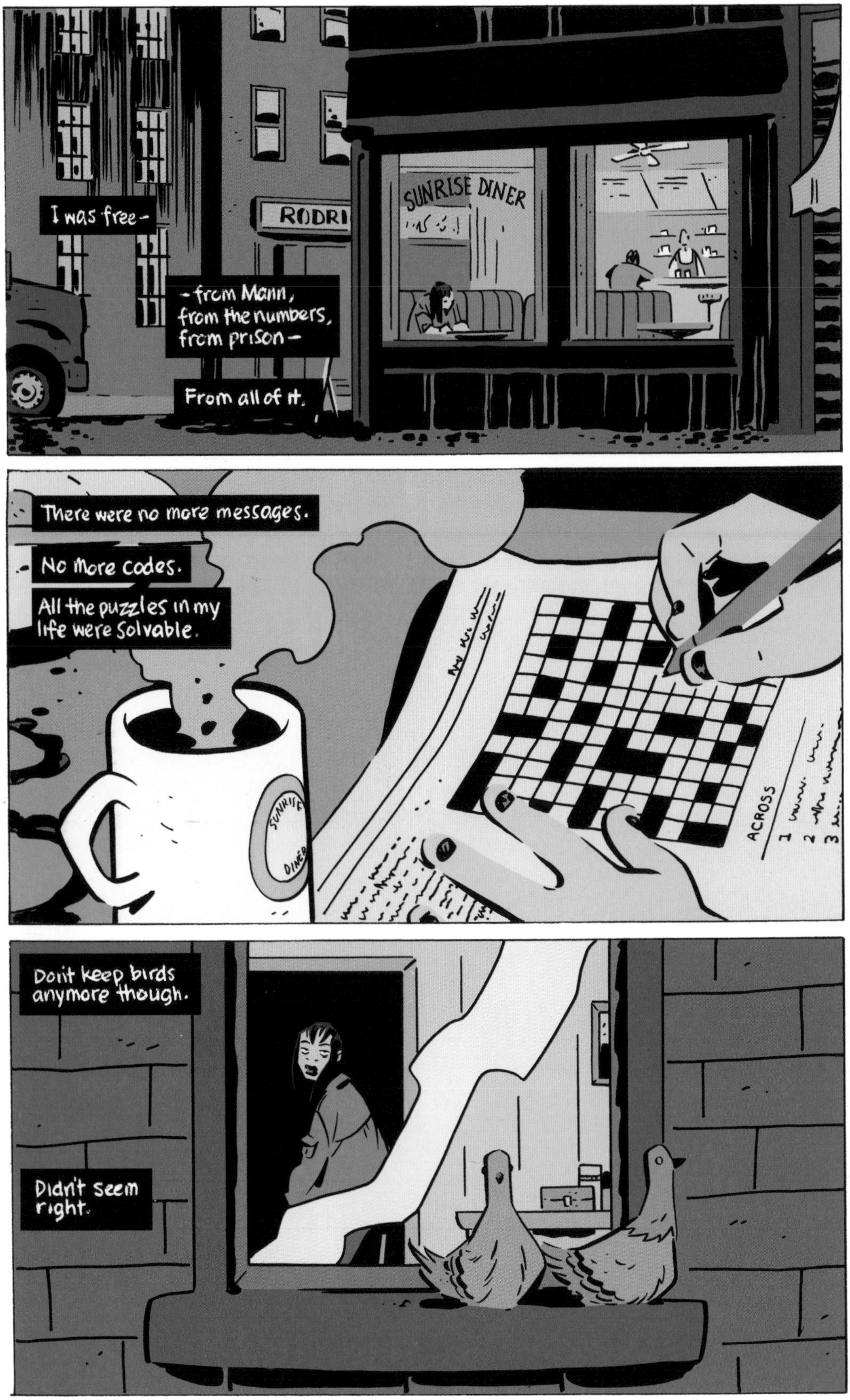

I was free-
-from Mann, from the numbers, from prison-
From all of it.
RODRI
SUNRISE DINER
There were no more messages.
No more codes.
All the puzzles in my life were solvable.
SUNRISE DINER
ACROSS
Don't keep birds anymore though.
Didn't seem right.

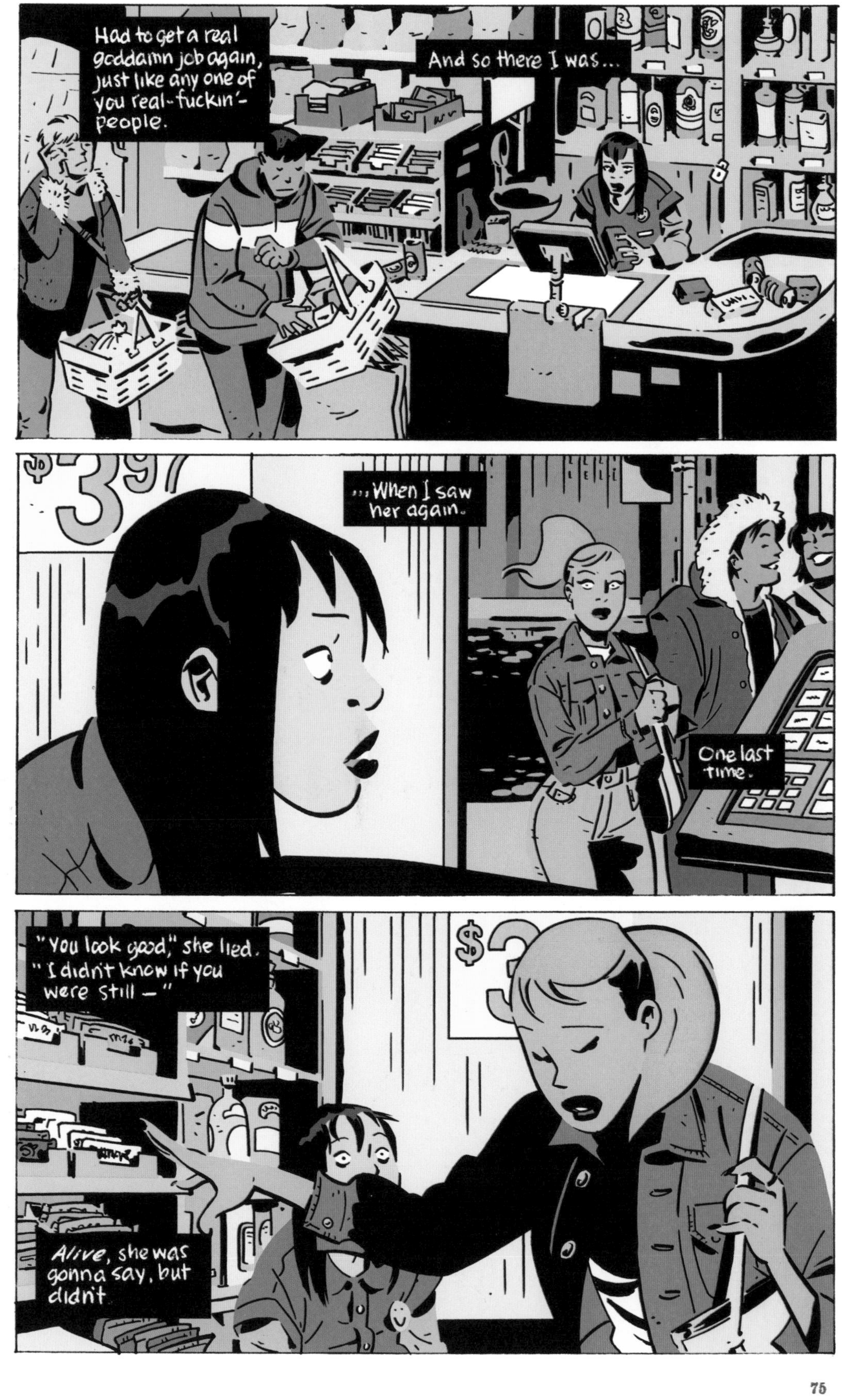
Had to get a real goddamn job again, just like any one of you real-fuckin'-people.
And so there I was...
...When I saw her again.
One last time.
"You look good," she lied. "I didn't know if you were still —"
Alive, she was gonna say, but didn't.

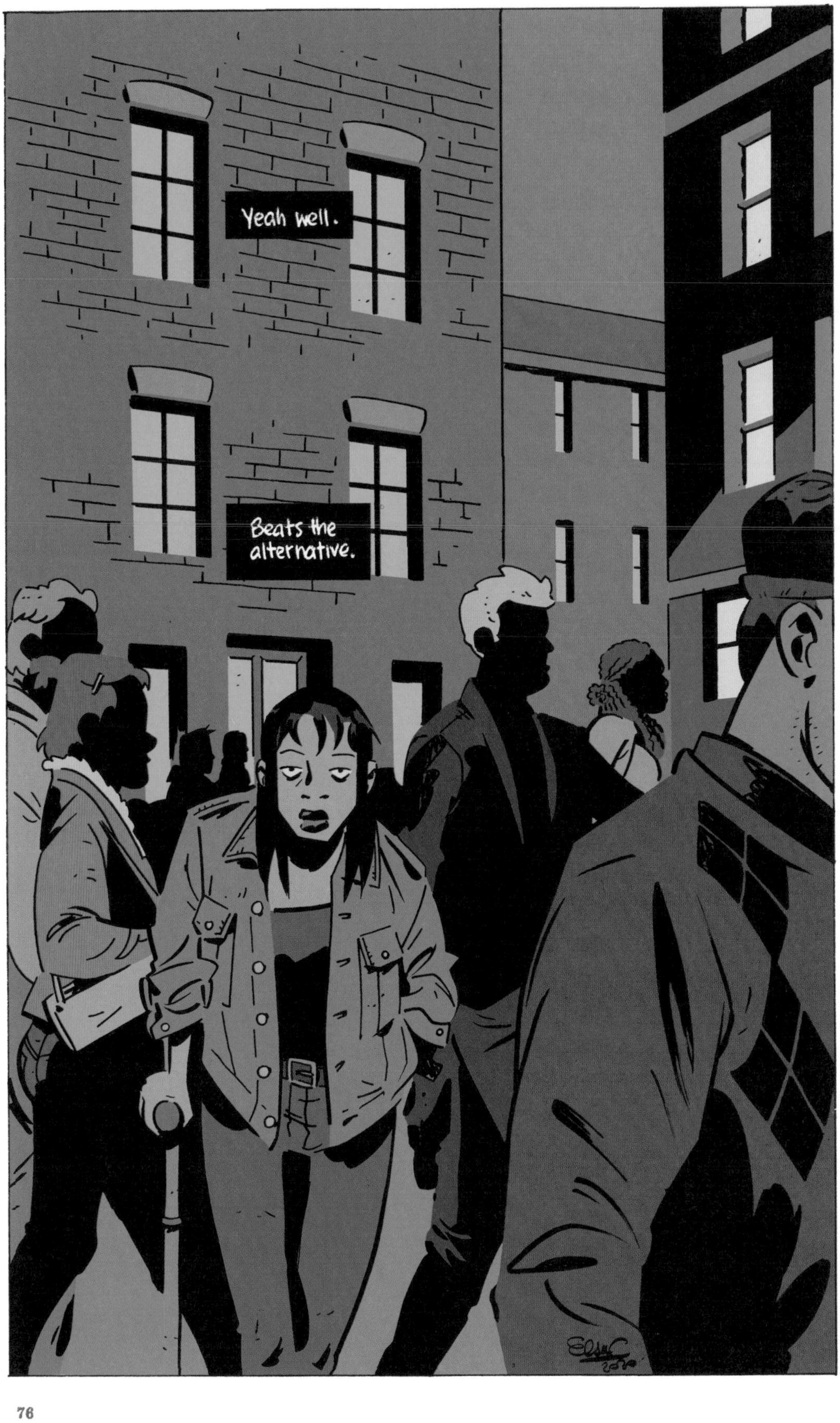
Yeah well.
Beats the alternative.

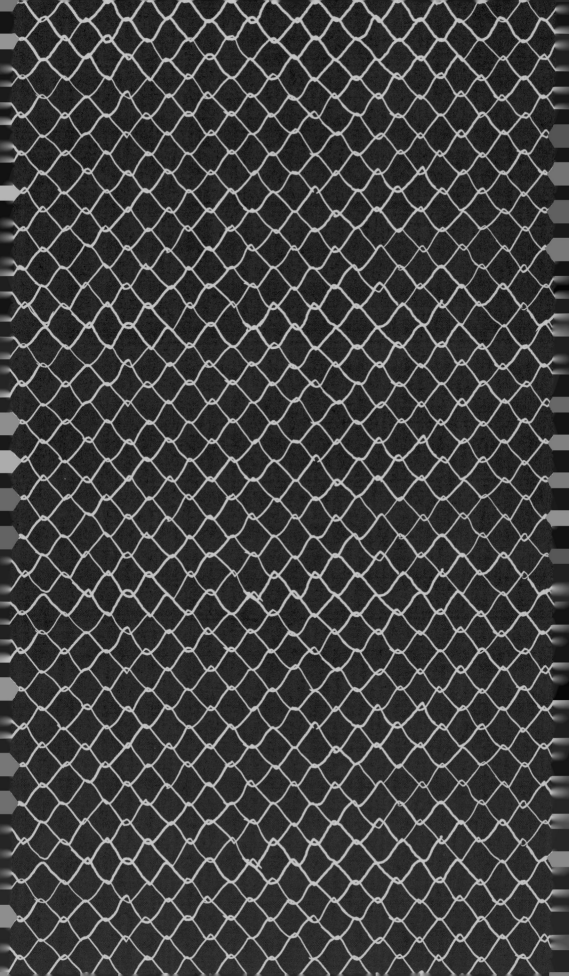

MATT FRACTION
WRITER

ELSA CHARRETIER
ARTIST

MATT HOLLINGSWORTH
COLORIST

KURT ANKENY
LETTERER

RIAN HUGHES
DESIGNER

DEANNA PHELPS
PRODUCTION

TURNER LOBEY
EDITOR

NOVEMBER CREATED BY
MATT FRACTION AND ELSA CHARRETIER

NOVEMBER, VOL. 4
First printing.
February 2021
Published by Image Comics, Inc.
Office of publication: 2701 NW Vaughn St., Suite 780, Portland, OR 97210.

Printed in CHINA.
For international rights,
contact: foreignlicensing@imagecomics.com.
ISBN: 978-1-5343-1821-2